**LAUGH OUT LOUD**

More Funny Stories for Children

*Also edited by Sara and Stephen Corrin*

STORIES FOR UNDER-FIVES
MORE STORIES FOR UNDER-FIVES
STORIES FOR SIX-YEAR-OLDS
STORIES FOR SEVEN-YEAR-OLDS
MORE STORIES FOR SEVEN-YEAR-OLDS
STORIES FOR EIGHT-YEAR-OLDS
STORIES FOR NINE-YEAR-OLDS
STORIES FOR TEN-YEAR-OLDS
IMAGINE THAT! FIFTEEN FANTASTIC TALES
PET STORIES FOR CHILDREN
THE FABER BOOK OF CHRISTMAS STORIES
ROUND THE CHRISTMAS TREE
ONCE UPON A RHYME: 101 POEMS FOR YOUNG
CHILDREN
THE FABER BOOK OF MODERN FAIRY TALES
THE FABER BOOK OF FAVOURITE FAIRY TALES
A TIME TO LAUGH: FUNNY STORIES FOR CHILDREN

# LAUGH OUT LOUD
*More Funny Stories for Children*

edited by
## Sara and Stephen Corrin

illustrated by
## Gerald Rose

*faber and faber*

LONDON · BOSTON

*A Time to Laugh: Thirty Stories for Young Children*
first published in 1972
by Faber and Faber Limited
3 Queen Square London WC1N 3AU
Reprinted in 1975

A selection of these stories
first published in 1989 as
*Laugh Out Loud: More Funny Stories for Children*

Printed in Great Britain by Richard Clay Ltd, Bungay, Suffolk

A CIP record for this book is available from the British Library.

ISBN 0-571-14177-3

# Contents

# Acknowledgements

We are most grateful to the undermentioned publishers, authors and agents for permission to include the following stories:

André Deutsch Limited for 'The Ugsome Thing' from *Ten Tales of Shellover* by Ruth Ainsworth.

Chatto and Windus Limited for 'The Elephant's Picnic' from *Don't Blame Me* by Richard Hughes.

Barrie and Jenkins Limited for 'A Meal with a Magician' from *My Friend Mr Leakey* by J. B. S. Haldane.

Hodder and Stoughton Children's Books (formerly Brockhampton Press Ltd) for 'The Woman Who Always Argued' by Leila Berg.

Mrs George Bambridge and Macmillan and Co. for 'The Elephant's Child' from *Just So Stories* by Rudyard Kipling.

The E. Nesbit Estate and John Farquharson Limited for 'The Magician's Heart' by E. Nesbit.

David Higham Associates Limited for 'Can Men Be Such Fools as All That?' by Eleanor Farjeon.

Octopus Publishing Group Limited for 'Puss and Pup' from *Harum Scarum* by J. Čapek.

We should like to thank Mrs S. Stonebridge, Principal Children's Librarian, Royal Borough of Kensington and Chelsea, Mrs Mary Clunes, Children's Librarian, Golders Green Public Library, Hazel Wilkinson, Mary Junor, Schools Librarian, Barnet, and Eileen Leach, Children's Librarian, Watford Library, for their ever-willing and invaluable help and advice; and, of course, Phyllis Hunt of Faber and Faber for constant guidance and encouragement.

# A Note for the Story-teller

What makes children laugh out loud? Although as adults we tend to think that their sense of humour is cruder and simpler than ours, closer analysis suggests that the basic stuff of humour is the same for child and adult alike: the little person outwitting the braggart and bully; the supercilious and haughty brought to justice; the theme of 'the smile on the face of the tiger'; slapstick; sweet revenge as in the Brer Rabbit stories; greed thwarted by elegant cunning as in 'The Little Hare and the Tiger'; the victim of the heavy hand of authority hitting back, as when the Elephant's Child spanks all his relatives with his newly found trunk. Nothing delights children more than the moment when he picks up his hairy uncle, the baboon, by one hairy leg and throws him into a hornet's nest.

The nagging wife theme, recurrent in folktale, where woman receives her come-uppance, is counterbalanced in other tales when the wife becomes the heroine, her cunning and wit helping her husband out of a scrape. Absurdity is a source of humour: the habitually contradictory wife in 'The Woman Who Always Argued' falls into a river during an argument with her husband and is eventually found floating *up* stream instead of *down*. So is the theme of the woman with the patience of a Job who turns the tables on her tormentor, as happens in 'The Ugsome Thing'.

The appeal to the child's rough sense of justice finds a never-failing response. Magic takes care of the implausibility of events in 'The Magician's Heart' when the wicked magician gets his just deserts and the Princess gets her Prince. The outrageous improbability of a tortoise literally bringing a wily jackal to heel in 'The Wicked Little Jackal' is accepted with unquestioning glee.

Such is the stuff these tales are made of and such is the stuff that has made them survive.

# The Wonderful Tar-Baby

One day Brer Fox went to work and got him some tar, and mixed it with some turpentine, and fix up a contraption what he called a Tar-Baby, and he took this here Tar-Baby and set her in the big road; and then he lay off in the bushes for to see what the news was going to be. And he didn't have to wait long, neither, 'cause by and by here comes Brer Rabbit, pacing down the road – lippity-clippity, clippity-lippity – just as saucy as a jay-bird. Brer Fox, he lay low. Brer Rabbit came prancing along till he spy the Tar-Baby, and then he fetched up on his behind legs like he was 'stonished. The Tar-Baby, she sat there, she did, and Brer Fox, he lay low.

'Morning!' says Brer Rabbit, says he – 'Nice weather, this morning,' says he.

Tar-Baby ain't saying nothing, and Brer Fox, he lay low.

'How are your symptoms this morning?' says Brer Rabbit, says he.

Brer Fox, he wink his eye slow, and lay low, and the Tar-Baby, she ain't saying nothing.

1

'How you come on then? Is you deaf?' says Brer
Rabbit, says he. "Cause if you is, I can holler louder,'
says he.

Tar-Baby stay still, and Brer Fox, he lay low.

'You're stuck up, that's what you is,' says Brer
Rabbit, says he, 'and I'm going to cure you, that's
what I'm a-going to do,' says he.

2

Brer Fox, he sort of chuckle in his stomach, but Tar-Baby ain't saying nothing.

'I'm going to learn you how to talk to 'spectable folks, if it's the last act I do,' says Brer Rabbit, says he. 'If you don't take off that hat and tell me howdy, I'm going to bust you wide open,' says he.

Tar-Baby stay still, and Brer Fox, he lay low.

Brer Rabbit keep on asking him, and the Tar-Baby, she keep on saying nothing, till presently Brer Rabbit draw back with his fist, he did, and blip! he took her on the side of the head. His fist stuck and he can't pull loose. The tar held him. But Tar-Baby, she stay still, and Brer Fox, he lay low.

'If you don't let me loose, I'll knock you again,' says Brer Rabbit, says he, and with that he fetch her a wipe with the other hand, and that stuck. Tar-Baby, she ain't saying nothing, and Brer Fox, he lay low.

'Turn me loose, before I kick the natural stuffing out of you,' says Brer Rabbit, says he, but the Tar-Baby, she ain't saying nothing. She just held on, and then Brer Rabbit lose the use of his feet the same way. Brer Fox, he lay low. Then Brer Rabbit squall out that if the Tar-Baby don't turn him loose, he butt her lop-sided. And then he butted, and his head got stuck. Then Brer Fox, he sauntered forth, looking just as innocent as a mocking-bird.

'Howdy, Brer Rabbit,' says Brer Fox, says he. 'You look sort of stuck-up this morning,' says he, and then

3

he rolled on the ground, and laughed and laughed until he couldn't laugh no more.

And that's how Brer Fox got the better of Brer Rabbit. Now you will hear how Brer Rabbit got his revenge.

# Brer Rabbit He's a Good Fisherman

One day, when Brer Rabbit, and Brer Fox, and Brer Coon, and Brer Bear and a whole lot of them was clearing a new ground for to plant a roasting-pear patch, the sun began to get sort of hot, and Brer Rabbit, he got tired; but he didn't let on, 'cause he feared the others would call him lazy, and he keep on carrying away rubbish and piling it up, till by and by he holler out that he got a thorn in his hand, and then he take and slip off and hunt for a cool place to rest. After a while he come across a well with a bucket hanging in it.

'That looks cool,' says Brer Rabbit, says he. 'And cool I 'specs she is. I'll just about get in there and take a nap,' and with that, in he jump, he did, and he ain't no sooner fix himself than the bucket begin to go down. Brer Rabbit, he was mighty scared. He know where he come from, but he don't know where he's going. Suddenly he feel the bucket hit the water, and there she sat, but Brer Rabbit, he keep mighty

5

still, 'cause he don't know what minute's going to be the next. He just lay there and shook and shiver.

Brer Fox always got one eye on Brer Rabbit, and when he slip off from the new ground, Brer Fox, he sneak after him. He knew Brer Rabbit was after some project or another, and he took and crope off, he did, and watch him. Brer Fox see Brer Rabbit come to the top of the well and stop, and then he see him jump in the bucket, and then, lo and behold! he see him go down out of sight. Brer Fox was the most 'stonished fox that you ever laid eyes on. He sat down in the bushes and thought and thought, but he don't make no head nor tails of this kind of business. Then he say to himself, says he:

'Well, if this don't beat everything!' says he. 'Right down there in that well Brer Rabbit keep his money hid, and if it ain't that, he done gone and 'scovered a gold mine, and if it ain't that, then I'm a-going to see what's in there,' says he.

Brer Fox crope up a little nearer, he did, and listen, but he don't hear no fuss, and he keep on getting nearer, and yet he don't hear nothing. By and by he get up close and peep down, but he don't see nothing, and he don't hear nothing. All this time Brer Rabbit was mighty near scared out of his skin, and he feared for to move 'cause the bucket might keel over and spill him out in the water. While he saying his prayers over and over, old Brer Fox holler out:

'Heyo, Brer Rabbit! Who you visitin' down there?' says he.

'Who? Me? Oh, I'm just a-fishing, Brer Fox,' says Brer Rabbit, says he. 'I just say to myself that I'd sort of s'prise you all with a mess of fishes, and so here I is, and there's the fishes. I'm a-fishing for supper, Brer Fox,' says Brer Rabbit, says he.

'Is there many of them down there, Brer Rabbit?' say Brer Fox, says he.

'Lots of them, Brer Fox; scores and scores of them. The water is naturally alive with them. Come down and help me haul them in, Brer Fox,' says Brer Rabbit, says he.

'How I going to get down, Brer Rabbit?'

'Jump into the other bucket, Brer Fox. It'll fetch you down all safe and sound.'

Brer Rabbit talked so happy and talked so sweet that Brer Fox he jump in the bucket, he did, and so he went down, 'cause his weight pulled Brer Rabbit up. When they pass one another on the half-way ground, Brer Rabbit he sing out:

> *'Good-bye, Brer Fox, take care o' your clothes,*
> *For this is the way the world goes;*
> *Some goes up and some goes down,*
> *You'll get to the bottom all safe and soun'.'*

When Brer Rabbit got out, he gallop off and told the folks what the well belonged to, that Brer Fox was down there muddying up the drinking water, and then he gallop back to the well, and holler down to Brer Fox:

> *'Here come a man with a great big gun –*
> *When he haul you up, you jump and run.'*

Well, soon enough Brer Fox was out of the well,

and in just about half an hour both of them was back on the new ground working just as if they'd never heard of no well. But every now and then Brer Rabbit would burst out laughing, and old Brer Fox would scowl and say nothing.

# Giacco and His Bean

Giacco was all alone in the world. The only thing he had was a cupful of beans, and one of these he used to eat each day until finally there was only one left.

'I won't eat this bean,' said Giacco. 'I'll put it in my pocket and perhaps it will bring me good luck.'

So he set out on his journeys, singing and whistling merrily to keep his spirits up, until he arrived at a quaint little house made of wood and china. He knocked at the door and a strange old man with a silver beard came and asked what he wanted.

'If you please, sir,' said Giacco politely, 'I have no father or mother and I have nothing to eat except this one bean which I keep hidden in my pocket to bring me luck.'

'You poor lad,' said the strange old man. He gave Giacco six walnuts to eat and let him sleep in his kitchen for the night. But during the night, Giacco's bean rolled out of his pocket and the strange old man's cat ate it up.

Giacco woke in the morning to find no bean in his pocket. He said to the old man, 'Kind sir, my bean has disappeared from my pocket. Whatever shall I do?'

'My naughty cat must have eaten it up,' said the old man. 'He's a wicked animal. You may take him with you on your journeys.'

Giacco thanked the old man and continued on his way with the wicked cat. Towards nightfall he arrived at a house made of paper and tin. He knocked at the door and a funny little woman came out and asked him what he wanted.

'I have no father or mother,' replied Giacco. 'I've only got this wicked cat that ate my good-luck bean.'

'You poor thing,' said the funny little woman. She gave him ten cherries to eat and let him sleep the night in her back-parlour. During the night the funny little woman's dog came and ate the cat and in the morning Giacco told her about it.

'That dog is a nasty brute. You can take it with you on your journeys,' said the funny little woman.

So Giacco set off once more with the brute of a dog until towards evening he arrived at a house made of cardboard and feathers. When he knocked at the door, a bald-headed man came and asked him what he wanted.

'I've no father or mother,' said Giacco, 'only this brute of a dog that ate the cat that ate my good-luck bean.'

'I'm very sorry to hear your bad news,' said the bald-headed man. He gave Giacco three apples to eat and let him sleep the night in his pig sty.

But during the night the pig ate the dog and in the morning Giacco told the bald-headed man that his dog had disappeared.

'It must have been that disgusting pig of mine. You can have him to accompany you on your journeys.'

So Giacco continued his travels with the pig trotting behind him.

As it grew dark he came to a tiny house made of baskets and straw. He called out through a hole in the straw and a tall girl with long flaxen plaits came and asked him what he wanted.

'I have no father or mother,' said Giacco, 'only this pig that ate the dog that ate the cat that ate my good-luck bean.'

'Sad,' said the tall girl, 'very sad.' And she gave him a juicy peach to eat and let him sleep the night in the stable.

During the night the horse ate the pig and when Giacco awoke in the morning he cried out, 'Hi! my pig has disappeared!'

'That must have been that silly horse of mine,' said the flaxen-plaited maiden. 'I'll have nothing more to do with him. Take him with you on your journeys.'

So Giacco rode off on the horse and he travelled quite a long way until he arrived at a castle. He banged the big iron knocker on the gate and a great big soldier came to ask what he wanted.

'My name is Giacco,' said the boy. 'I have no father or mother. All I have in the world is this horse that

ate the pig that ate the dog that ate the cat that ate my good-luck bean.'

'Ha! Ha! Ha!' laughed the soldier, 'Ha! Ha! Ha! Ha! Ha! Ha! Jolly good! Jolly good! I must go and tell the King.'

'Ha! Ha! Ha! Ho! Ho! Ho!' laughed the King. 'That's the most comical story I have ever heard. Ha! Ha! Ha! Ho! Ho! Ho! Fancy a bean eating a dog that ate a horse that ate a pig! Ha! Ha! Ha! Ho! Ho! Ho!'

'If you will permit me to correct Your Majesty,' said Giacco, making a low bow, 'it wasn't quite like that. It was the horse that ate the pig that ate the dog that ate the cat that ate my good-luck bean.'

'My mistake,' said the King, 'ho! ho! You are quite

right, young man. It was the pig that ate the horse, no, I mean it was the bean that ate the pig, no, it was . . . ' and he went off again into a great peal of laughter. And all the lords and ladies in the court began to laugh and the cooks in the kitchens began to laugh and the grooms in the stables and the soldiers outside in the yard and then the people outside in the streets . . . And soon the whole kingdom was roaring with laughter.

'Look here, Giacco,' said the King when he had managed to get his breath. 'If you tell me this story about your good-luck bean eating the dog, no, I mean about the pig eating the horse, no . . . well you know what I mean, young man. If you tell me that story every day, you can sit on a throne next to me and wear a golden crown and be treated just like me. Ha! Ha! Ha! Ho! Ho! Ho!'

And everybody burst into huge peals of laughter all over again, and Giacco lived happily ever after.

# The Horse and the Lion

The lion was hungry. Hunting hadn't been too good during the past week. He was sitting by the roadside feeling sorry for himself when a handsome horse came trotting past. The lion's mouth watered as he thought what a wonderful dinner the horse would make if only he could catch him. The lion couldn't get his mind off that horse. So he let it be noised about that he had become a wonderful doctor who could heal any animal's complaint.

A day or two later the horse, pretending that he had a thorn in his hoof, came to the lion's den for help. The lion licked his chops. This was the chance he had been looking for. He asked the horse to raise one of his hind feet so that he could make an examination. Solicitously, in his best bedside manner, he bent his head as though to examine the ailing hoof. Just as the lion was ready to spring, the horse let go with his upraised hoof. There was a sickening thud as hoof met nose. And the last thing the lion remembered was a whinny of laughter as the horse galloped away towards the forest.

# A Meal with a Magician

I have had some very odd meals in my time, and if I liked I could tell you about a meal in a mine, or a meal in Moscow, or a meal with a millionaire. But I think you will be more interested to hear about a meal I had one evening with a magician, because it is more unusual. People don't often have a meal of that sort, for rather few people know a magician at all well, because there aren't very many in England. Of course, I am talking about real magicians. Some conjurors call themselves magicians, and they are very clever men. But they can't do the sort of things that real magicians do. I mean, a conjuror can turn a rabbit into a bowl of goldfish, but it's always done under cover or behind something, so that you can't see just what is happening. But a real magician can turn a cow into a grandfather clock with people looking on all the time. Only it is very much harder work, and no one could do it twice a day, and six days a week, like a conjuror does with rabbits.

When I first met Mr Leakey I never guessed he was a magician. I met him like this. I was going

18

across the Haymarket about five o'clock one afternoon. When I got to the refuge by a lamp-post in the
middle I stopped, but a little man who had crossed
so far with me went on. Then he saw a motor-bus
going down the hill and jumped back, which is
always a silly thing to do. He jumped right in front
of a car, and if I hadn't grabbed his overcoat collar
and pulled him back on to the refuge, I think the
car would have knocked him down. For it was wet
weather, and the road was very greasy, so it only
skidded when the driver put the brakes on.

The little man was very grateful, but dreadfully
frightened, so I gave him my arm across the street,
and saw him back to his home, which was quite near.
I won't tell you where it was, because if I did you
might go there and bother him, and if he got really
grumpy it might be very awkward indeed for you. I
mean, he might make some of your ears as big as a
cabbage-leaf, or turn your hair green, or exchange
your right and left feet, or something like that. And
then everyone who saw you would burst out laughing, and say, 'Here comes wonky Willie, or lop-sided
Lizzie,' or whatever your name is.

'I can't bear modern traffic,' he said, 'the motor-
buses make me so frightened. If it wasn't for my
work in London I should like to live on a little island
where there are no roads, or on the top of a moun-
tain, or somewhere like that.' The little man was sure
I had saved his life, and insisted on my having dinner
with him, so I said I would come to dinner on

19

Wednesday week. I didn't notice anything specially odd about him then, except that his ears were rather large and that he had a little tuft of hair on the top of each of them, rather like the lynx at the zoo. I remember I thought if I had hair there I would shave it off. He told me that his name was Leakey, and that he lived on the first floor.

Well, on Wednesday week I went to dinner with him. I went upstairs in a block of flats and knocked at a quite ordinary door, and the little hall of the flat was quite ordinary too, but when I got inside it was one of the oddest rooms I have ever seen. Instead of wallpaper there were curtains round it, embroidered with pictures of people and animals. There was a picture of two men building a house, and another of a man with a dog and a cross-bow hunting rabbits. I know they were made of embroidery, because I touched them, but it must have been a very funny sort of embroidery, because the pictures were always changing. As long as you looked at them they stayed still, but if you looked away and back again they had altered. During dinner the builders had put a fresh storey on the house, the hunter had shot a bird with his cross-bow, and his dog had caught two rabbits.

The furniture was very funny, too. There was a bookcase made out of what looked like glass with the largest books in it that I ever saw, none of them less than a foot high, and bound in leather. There were cupboards running along the tops of the book-shelves. The chairs were beautifully carved, with high wooden backs, and there were two tables. One was made of copper, and had a huge crystal globe on it. The other was a solid lump of wood about ten feet long, four feet wide, and three feet high, with holes cut in it so that you could get your knees under it. There were various odd things hanging from the ceiling. At first I couldn't make out how the room was lit. Then I saw that the light came from plants of a sort I had never seen before, growing in pots. They had red, yellow and blue fruits as big as tomatoes, which shone. They weren't disguised electric lamps, for I touched one and it was quite cold and soft like a fruit.

'Well,' said Mr Leakey, 'what would you like for dinner?'

'Oh, whatever you've got,' I said.

'You can have whatever you like,' he said. 'Please choose a soup.'

So I thought he probably got his dinner from a restaurant, and I said, 'I'll have a Bortsch,' which is a red Russian soup with cream in it.

'Right,' he said, 'I'll get it ready. Look here, do you mind if we have dinner served the way mine usually is? You aren't easily frightened, are you?'

'Not very easily,' I said.

'All right, then, I'll call my servant, but I warn you he's rather odd.'

At that Mr Leakey flapped the tops and lobes of his ears against his head. It made a noise like when one claps one's hands, but not so loud. Out of a large

21

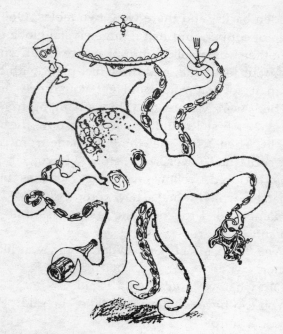

copper pot about as big as the copper you wash
clothes in, which was standing in one corner, came
what at first I thought was a large wet snake. Then
I saw it had suckers all down one side, and was really
the arm of an octopus. This arm opened a cupboard
and pulled out a large towel with which it wiped the
next arm that came out. The dry arm then clung on
to the wall with its suckers, and gradually the whole
beast came out, dried itself, and crawled up the wall.
It was the largest octopus I have ever seen; each arm
was about eight feet long, and its body was as big as
a sack. It crawled up the wall, and then along the

ceiling, holding on by its suckers like a fly. When it got above the table it held on by one arm only, and with the other seven got plates and knives and forks out of the cupboards above the bookshelves and laid the table with them.

'That's my servant Oliver,' said Mr Leakey. 'He's much better than a person, because he has more arms to work with, and he can hold on to a plate with about ten suckers, so he never drops one.'

When Oliver the octopus had laid the table we sat down and he offered me a choice of water, lemonade, beer, and four different kinds of wine with his seven free arms, each of which held a different bottle. I chose some water and some very good wine from Burgundy.

All this was so odd that I was not surprised to notice that my host was wearing a top hat, but I certainly did think it a little queer when he took it off and poured two platefuls of soup out of it.

'Ah, we want some cream,' he added. 'Come here, Phyllis.' At this a small green cow, about the size of a rabbit, ran out of a hutch, jumped on to the table, and stood in front of Mr Leakey, who milked her into a silver cream jug which Oliver had handed down for the purpose. The cream was excellent, and I enjoyed the soup very much.

'What would you like next?' said Mr Leakey.

'I leave it to you,' I answered.

'All right,' he said, 'we'll have grilled turbot, and

23

turkey to follow. Catch us a turbot, please, Oliver, and be ready to grill it, Pompey.'

At this Oliver picked up a fish-hook with the end of one of his arms and began making casts in the air like a fly-fisher. Meanwhile I heard a noise in the fireplace, and Pompey came out. He was a small dragon about a foot long, not counting his tail, which measured another foot. He had been lying on the burning coals, and was red-hot. So I was glad to see that as soon as he got out of the fire he put a pair of asbestos boots which were lying in the fender on to his hind feet.

'Now, Pompey,' said Mr Leakey, 'hold your tail up properly. If you burn the carpet again, I'll pour a bucket of cold water over you. (Of course, I wouldn't really do that; it's very cruel to pour cold water on a dragon, especially a little one with a thin skin),' he added in a low voice, which only I could hear. But poor Pompey took the threat quite seriously. He whimpered, and the yellow flames which were coming out of his nose turned a dull blue. He waddled along rather clumsily on his hind legs, holding up his tail and the front part of his body. I think the asbestos boots made walking rather difficult for him, though they saved the carpet, and no doubt kept his hind feet warm. But of course dragons generally walk on all four feet and seldom wear boots, so I was surprised that Pompey walked as well as he did.

I was so busy watching Pompey that I never saw

how Oliver caught the turbot, and by the time I looked up at him again he had just finished cleaning it, and threw it down to Pompey. Pompey caught it in his front paws, which had cooled down a bit, and were just about the right temperature for grilling things. He had long thin fingers with claws on the end; and held the fish on each hand alternately, holding the other against his red-hot chest to warm it. By the time he had finished and put the grilled fish on to a plate which Oliver handed down, Pompey was clearly feeling the cold, for his teeth were chattering, and he scampered back to the fire with evident joy.

'Yes,' said Mr Leakey, 'I know some people say it is cruel to let a young dragon cool down like that, and liable to give it a bad cold. But I say a dragon can't begin to learn too soon that life isn't all fire and flames, and the world is a colder place than he'd like it to be. And they don't get colds if you give them plenty of sulphur to eat. Of course, a dragon with a cold is an awful nuisance to itself and everyone else. I've known one throw flames for a hundred yards when it sneezed. But that was a full-grown one, of course. It burned down one of the Emperor of China's palaces. Besides, I really couldn't afford to keep a dragon if I didn't make use of him. Last week, for example, I used his breath to burn the old paint off the door, and his tail makes quite a good soldering iron. Then he's really much more reliable than a dog for dealing with burglars. They might shoot a dog, but leaden bullets just melt the moment they touch

25

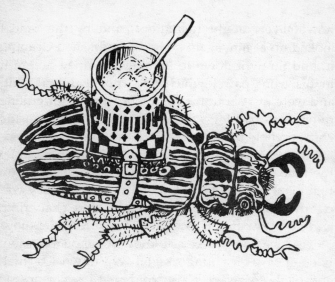

Pompey. Anyway, I think dragons were meant for use, not ornament. Don't you?'

'Well, do you know,' I answered, 'I am ashamed to say that Pompey is the first live dragon I've ever seen.'

'Of course,' said Mr Leakey, 'how stupid of me. I have so few guests here except professional colleagues that I forgot you were a layman. By the way,' he went on, as he poured sauce out of his hat over the fish, 'I don't know if you've noticed anything queer about this dinner. Of course, some people are more observant than others.'

'Well,' I answered, 'I've never seen anything like it before.'

For example, at that moment I was admiring an

26

enormous rainbow-coloured beetle which was crawling towards me over the table with a salt-cellar strapped on its back.

'Ah well then,' said my host, 'perhaps you have guessed that I'm a magician. Pompey, of course, is a real dragon, but most of the other animals here were people before I made them what they are now. Take Oliver, for example. When he was a man he had his legs cut off by a railway train. I couldn't stick them on again because my magic doesn't work against machinery. Poor Oliver was bleeding to death, so I thought the only way to save his life was to turn him into some animal with no legs. Then he couldn't have any legs to have been cut off. I turned him into a snail, and took him home in my pocket. But whenever I tried to turn him back into something more interesting, like a dog, it had no hind legs. But an octopus has really got no legs. Those eight tentacles grow out of its head. So when I turned him into an octopus, he was all right. And he had been a waiter when he was a man, so he soon learned his job. I think he's much better than a maid because he can lift the plates from above, and doesn't stand behind one and breathe down one's neck. You may have the rest of the fish, Oliver, and a bottle of beer. I know that's what you like.'

Oliver seized the fish in one of his arms and put it into an immense beak like a parrot's but much bigger, which lay in the centre of the eight arms. Then he took a bottle of beer out of a cupboard, unscrewed the cork with his beak, hoisted himself up to the ceiling with two of his other arms, and turned over so that his mouth was upwards. As he emptied the bottle he winked one of his enormous eyes. Then I felt sure he must really be a man, for I never saw an ordinary octopus wink.

The turkey came in a more ordinary way. Oliver let down a large hot plate, and then a dish-cover on to it. There was nothing in the cover, as I could see. Mr Leakey got up, took a large wand out of the umbrella stand, pointed it at the dish-cover, said a few words, and there was the turkey steaming hot when Oliver lifted the cover off it.

'Of course, that's easy,' said Mr Leakey, 'any good conjuror could do it, but you can never be sure the food you get in that way is absolutely fresh. That's why I like to see my fish caught. But birds are all the better for being a few days old. Ah, we shall want some sausages too. That's easy.'

He took a small clay pipe out of his pocket and blew into it. A large brown bubble came out of the other end, shaped like a sausage. Oliver picked it off with the end of one of his tentacles, and put it on a hot plate, and it was a sausage, because I ate it. He made six sausages in this way, and while I was watching him Oliver had handed down the vegetables. I don't know where he got them. The sauce and gravy came out of Mr Leakey's hat, as usual.

Just after this the only accident of the evening happened. The beetle who carried the salt-cellar round tripped over a fold in the tablecloth and spilled the salt just in front of Mr Leakey, who spoke to him very angrily.

'It's lucky for you, Leopold, that I'm a sensible man. If I were superstitious, which I'm not, I should think I was going to have bad luck. But it's you who are going to have bad luck, if anyone. I've a good mind to turn you back into a man, and if I do, I'll put you straight on to that carpet and send you to the nearest police station; and when the police ask you where you've been hiding, d'you think they'll believe you when you say you've been a beetle for the last year? Are you sorry?'

Leopold, with a great struggle, got out of his harness and rolled on to his back, feebly waving his legs in the air like a dog does when he's ashamed of himself.

'When Leopold was a man,' said Mr Leakey, 'he made money by swindling people. When the police found it out and were going to arrest him, he came to me for help, but I thought it served him right. So I said, "If they catch you, you'll get sent to penal servitude for seven years. If you like I'll turn you into a beetle for five years, which isn't so long, and then, if you've been a good beetle, I'll make you into a man with a different sort of face, so the police won't know you." So now Leopold is a beetle. Well, I see he's sorry for spilling the salt. Now, Leopold, you must pick up all the salt you've spilt.'

He turned Leopold over on his front and I watched

29

him begin to pick the salt up. It took him over an hour. First he picked it up a grain at a time in his mouth, lifted himself on his front legs, and dropped it into the salt-cellar. Then he thought of a better plan. He was a beetle of the kind whose feelers are short and spread out into a fan. He started shovelling the salt with his feelers, and got on much quicker that way. But fairly soon he got uncomfortable. His feelers started to itch or something, and he had to wipe them with his legs. Finally he got a bit of paper and used it for a shovel, holding it with his front feet.

'That's very clever for a beetle,' said my host. 'When I turn him back into a man he'll be quite good with his hands, and I expect he'll be able to earn his living at an honest job.'

As we were finishing the turkey, Mr Leakey looked up anxiously from time to time.

'I hope Abdu'l Makkar won't be late with the strawberries,' he said.

'Strawberries?' I asked in amazement, for it was the middle of January.

'Oh yes, I've sent Abdu'l Makkar, who is a jinn, to New Zealand for some. Of course, it's summer there. He oughtn't to be long now, if he has been good, but you know what jinns are, they have their faults, like the rest of us. Curiosity, especially. When one sends them on long errands they will fly too high. They like to get quite close to Heaven to over-hear what the angels are saying, and then the angels throw shooting stars at them. Then they drop their parcels, or come home half-scorched. He ought to be back soon, he's been away over an hour. Meanwhile we'll have some other fruit, in case he's late.'

He got up, and tapped the four corners of the table with his wand. At each corner the wood swelled; then it cracked, and a little green shoot came out and started growing. In a minute they were already about a foot high, with several leaves at the top, and the bottom quite woody. I could see from the leaves that one was a cherry, another a pear, and the third a peach, but I didn't know the fourth.

As Oliver was clearing away the remains of the turkey with four of his arms and helping himself to a sausage with a fifth, Abdu'l Makkar came in. He came feet first through the ceiling, which seemed to close behind him like water in the tank of the diving birds' house in the Zoo, when you look at it from underneath while a penguin dives in. It shook a little for a moment afterwards. He narrowly missed one of Oliver's arms, but alighted safely on the floor, bending his knees to break his fall, and bowing deeply to Mr Leakey. He had a brown face with rather a long nose, and looked like a man, except that he had a pair of leathery wings folded on his back, and his nails were of gold. He wore a turban and clothes of green silk.

'O peacock of the world and redresser of injustices,' he said, 'thy unworthy servant comes into the presence with rare and refreshing fruit.'

'The presence deigns to express gratification at the result of thy labours.'

'The joy of thy negligible slave is as the joy of King Solomon, son of David (on whom be peace, if he has not already obtained peace) when he first beheld Balkis, the Queen of Sheba. May the Terminator of Delights and Separator of Companions be far from this dwelling.'

'May the Deluder of Intelligence never trouble the profundity of thine apprehension.'

'O Dominator of Demons and Governor of Goblins, what Egregious Enchanter or Noble Necromancer graces thy board?'

'It is written, O Abdu'l Makkar, in the book of the sayings of the prophet Shoaib, the apostle of the Midianites, that curiosity slew the cat of Pharaoh, King of Egypt.'

'That is a true word.'

'Thy departure is permitted. Awaken me at the accustomed hour. But stay! My safety razor hath no more blades and the shops of London are closed. Fly therefore to Montreal, where it is even now high noon, and purchase me a packet thereof.'

'I tremble and obey.'

'Why dost thou tremble, O audacious among the Ifreets?'

'O Emperor of Enchantment, the lower air is full of aeroplanes, flying swifter than a magic carpet, and each making a din like unto the bursting of the great dam of Sheba, and the upper air is infested with meteorites.'

'Fly therefore at a height of five miles and thou shalt avoid both the one peril and the other. And now, O Performer of Commands and Executor of Behests, thou hast my leave to depart.'

'May the wisdom of Plato, the longevity of Shiqq, the wealth of Solomon, and the success of Alexander, be thine.'

'The like unto thee, with brazen knobs thereon.'

The jinn now vanished, this time through the floor. While he and Mr Leakey had been talking the trees had grown up to about four feet high, and flowered. The flowers were now falling off, and little green fruits were swelling.

'You have to talk like that to a jinn or you lose his respect. I hope you don't mind my not introducing you, but really jinns may be quite awkward at times,' said my host. 'Of course, Abdu'l Makkar is a nice chap and means well, but he might be very embarrassing to you, as you don't know the Word of Power to send him away. For instance, if you were playing cricket and went in against a fast bowler, he'd probably turn up and ask you, "Shall I slay thine enemy, O Defender of Stumps, or merely convert him into a he-goat of loathsome appearance and afflicted with the mange?" You know, I used to be very fond of watching cricket, but I can't do it now. Quite a little magic will upset a match. Last year I went to see the Australians playing against Gloucester, and just

33

because I felt a little sympathetic with Gloucestershire the Australian wickets went down like ninepins. If I hadn't left before the end they'd have been beaten. And after that I couldn't go to any of the test matches. After all, one wants the best side to win.'

We next ate the New Zealand strawberries, which were very good, with Phyllis's cream. While we did so Pompey, who acted as a sort of walking stove, came out again and melted some cheese to make a Welsh rarebit. After this we went on to dessert. The fruit was now quite ripe. The fourth tree bore half a dozen golden fruits shaped rather like apricots, but much bigger, and my host told me they were mangoes, which of course usually grow in India. In fact you can't make them grow in England except by magic. So I said I would try a mango.

'Aha,' said Mr Leakey, 'this is where I have a pull over Lord Melchett or the Duke of Westminster, or any other rich man. They might be able to get mangoes here by aeroplane, but they couldn't give them as dessert at a smart dinner-party.'

'Why not?' I asked.

'That shows you've never eaten one. The only proper place to eat a mango is in your bath. You see, it has a tough skin and a squashy inside, so when once you get through the skin all the juice squirts out. And that would make a nasty mess of people's white shirts. D'you ever wear a stiff-fronted shirt?'

'Not often.'

'A good thing too. You probably don't know why

people wear them. It's a curious story. About a hundred years ago a great Mexican enchanter called Whiztopacoatl came over to Europe. And he got very annoyed with the rich men. He didn't so much mind their being rich but he thought they spent their money on such ugly things, and were dreadfully stodgy and smug. So he decided to turn them all into turtles. Now, to do that somebody has to say two different spells at the same time, which is pretty difficult, I can tell you. So Whiztopacoatl went round to an English sorcerer called Mr Benedict Barnacle, to borrow a two-headed parrot that belonged to him. It was rather like one of those two-headed eagles they used to have on the Russian and Austrian flags. Then he was going to teach one of the heads one spell, and the other head the second spell; and when the parrot said both at once all the rich men would have turned into turtles. But Mr Barnacle persuaded him to be less fierce, so finally they agreed that for a hundred years the rich men in Europe should be made to wear clothes only fit for turtles. Because of course the front of the turtle is stiff and flat, and it is the only sort of animal that would be quite comfortable in a shirt with a stiff flat front. They made a spell to stiffen all the shirts, and of course it worked very well, but it's wearing off now, and soon nobody will wear such silly clothes any more.

'About your mango; you can eat it quite safely, if you just wait a moment while I enchant it so that it won't splash over you.'

35

Quite a short spell and a little wiggling of his wand were enough, and then I ate a mango. It was wonderful. It was the only fruit I have ever eaten that was better than the best strawberries. I can't describe the flavour, which is a mixture of all sorts of things, including a little resin, like the smell of a pine forest in summer. There is a huge flattish stone in the middle, too big to get into your mouth, and all round it a squashy yellow pulp. To test the spell I tried to spill some down my waistcoat, but it merely jumped up into my mouth. Mr Leakey ate a pear, and gave me the other five mangoes to take home. But I had to eat them in my bath because they weren't enchanted.

While we were having coffee (out of the hat, of course) Mr Leakey rubbed one corner of the table with his wand and it began to sprout with very fine grass. When it was about as high as the grass on a lawn, he called Phyllis out of her hutch, and she ate some of it for her dinner. We talked for a while about magic, football, and the odder sorts of dog, such as Bedlington terriers and rough-haired Dachshunds, and then I said I must be getting home.

'I'll take you home,' said Mr Leakey, 'but when you have a day to spare you must come round and spend it with me, if you'd care to see the sort of things I generally do, and we might go over to India or Java or somewhere for the afternoon. Let me know when you're free. But now just stand on this carpet, and shut your eyes, because people often get giddy the first two or three times they travel by magic carpet.'

We got on to the carpet. I took a last look at the table, where Leopold had just finished picking up the salt, and was resting, while Phyllis was chewing the cud. Then I shut my eyes, my host told the carpet my address, flapped his ears, and I felt a rush of cold air on my cheeks, and a slight giddiness. Then the air was warm again. Mr Leakey told me to open my eyes, and I was in my sitting-room at home, five miles away. As the room is small, and there were a number of books and things on the floor, the carpet could not settle down properly, and stayed about a foot up in the air. Luckily it was quite stiff, so I stepped down off it, and turned the light on.

'Good-night,' said Mr Leakey, bending down to shake my hand, and then he flapped his ears and he and the carpet vanished. I was left in my room with nothing but a nice full feeling and a parcel of mangoes to persuade me that I had not been dreaming.

# The Elephant's Picnic

Elephants are generally clever animals, but there was once an elephant who was very silly; and his great friend was a kangaroo. Now, kangaroos are not often clever animals, and this one certainly was not, so she and the elephant got on very well together.

One day they thought they would like to go off for a picnic by themselves. But they did not know anything about picnics, and had not the faintest idea of what to do to get ready.

'What do you do on a picnic?' the elephant asked a child he knew.

'Oh, we collect wood and make a fire, and then we boil the kettle,' said the child.

'What do you boil the kettle for?' said the elephant in surprise.

'Why, for tea, of course,' said the child in a snapping sort of way; so the elephant did not like to ask any more questions. But he went and told the kangaroo, and they collected together all the things they thought they would need.

When they got to the place where they were going

to have their picnic, the kangaroo said that she would collect the wood because she had got a pouch to carry it back in. A kangaroo's pouch, of course, is very small; so the kangaroo carefully chose the smallest twigs she could find, and only about five or six of those. In fact, it took a lot of hopping to find any sticks small enough to go in her pouch at all; and it was a long time before she came back. But silly though the elephant was, he soon saw those sticks would not be enough for a fire.

'Now I will go off and get some wood,' he said.

His ideas of getting wood were different. Instead of taking little twigs he pushed down whole trees with his forehead, and staggered back to the picnic-place with them rolled up in his trunk. Then the kangaroo struck a match, and they lit a bonfire made of whole trees. The blaze, of course, was enormous, and the fire was so hot that for a long time they could not get near it; and it was not until it began to die down a bit that they were able to get near enough to cook anything.

'Now let's boil the kettle,' said the elephant. Amongst the things he had brought was a brightly shining copper kettle and a very large black iron saucepan. The elephant filled the saucepan with water.

'What are you doing that for?' said the kangaroo.

'To boil the kettle in, you silly,' said the elephant. So he popped the kettle in the saucepan of water, and put the saucepan on the fire; for he thought, the old juggins, that you boil a kettle in the same way you boil an egg, or boil a cabbage! And the kangaroo, of course, did not know any better.

So they boiled and boiled the kettle, and every now and then they prodded it with a stick.

'It doesn't seem to be getting tender,' said the elephant sadly, 'and I'm sure we can't eat it for tea until it does.'

So then away he went and got more wood for the fire; and still the saucepan boiled and boiled, and still the kettle remained as hard as ever. It was getting late now, almost dark.

'I'm afraid it won't be ready for tea,' said the kangaroo. 'I am afraid we shall have to spend the night here. I wish we had got something with us to sleep in.'

'Haven't you?' said the elephant. 'You mean to say you didn't pack before you came away?'

'No,' said the kangaroo. 'What should I have packed anyway?'

'Why, your trunk, of course,' said the elephant. 'That is what people pack.'

'But I haven't got a trunk,' said the kangaroo.

'Well, I have,' said the elephant, 'and I've packed it! Kindly pass the pepper; I want to unpack!'

So then the kangaroo passed the elephant the pepper, and the elephant took a good sniff. Then he gave a most tremendous sneeze, and everything he had packed in his trunk shot out of it – toothbrush, spare socks, gym shoes, a comb, a bag of bull's-eyes, his pyjamas, and his Sunday suit. So then the elephant put on his pyjamas and lay down to sleep; but the kangaroo had no pyjamas, and so, of course, she could not sleep.

'All right,' she said to the elephant; 'you sleep; and I will sit up and keep the fire going.'

So all night the kangaroo kept the fire blazing brightly and the kettle boiling merrily in the saucepan. When the next morning came the elephant woke up.

'Now,' he said, 'let's have our breakfast.'

So they took the kettle out of the saucepan; and what do you think? It was boiled as tender as tender could be! So they cut it fairly in half and shared it between them, and ate it for breakfast; and both agreed they had never had so good a breakfast in their lives.

# The Language of Animals

In the heart of Serbia lies a dark forest. Now this forest is enchanted, although the people who live round there don't know it.

One day a poor shepherd was driving his sheep along a path when he heard a peculiar hissing sound. As he came nearer he noticed a clump of bushes on fire and there, trapped in the flames, was a snake hissing and crying for help. The shepherd was a kind man and he could not but feel sorry for this poisonous reptile. But imagine his surprise when the snake addressed him in his own language. 'O Shepherd, do save me from this fire, I beseech you.' Quickly the shepherd stretched out his crook and the snake entwined itself around the stick. But to his horror, as soon as it was safe, the serpent uncoiled itself from the stick and crept around his arm and shoulders till he felt it almost throttling his neck. Trembling with fear the poor shepherd cried, 'Ungrateful wretch, are you going to kill me when I have saved your life?'

'Have no fear, my saviour,' hissed the snake

gently, 'just take me to my father's house; he is the snake king and will richly reward you for what you have done.' The shepherd was terrified at the thought of meeting the snake king and he tried to refuse, but the snake prince persuaded him, saying nothing would happen to his sheep while he was away and he would never regret his visit. So the poor

43

man left his sheep and crossed the enchanted forest with the snake still twisted round his neck, till they came to a fine palace built of golden beech leaves, with a gateway made of living serpents coiling and writhing about in fantastic patterns. But the snake prince hissed at them and they all untwined, so that the shepherd could pass in peace. Then the snake prince said to him, 'My father will offer you riches, gold, silver, precious stones – anything you wish. But don't be tempted by these; instead ask him to grant you the gift of understanding the language of animals. He may refuse you at first but in the end he will have to grant your request.'

They found the king, coiled, fast asleep on his throne of polished stone. His skin was shrivelled with age and on his crest he wore a crown of gold. Great was his joy when he awoke to find his beloved son beside him. When the snake prince told him how his life had been saved the king turned to the shepherd and asked him to name his own reward. The shepherd approached the throne fearfully and said timidly, 'My only wish is to be given the language of animals.' At this the king shook his head dolefully and answered:

'All my riches are at your disposal but I cannot grant your request. It is too dangerous for mere humans, for if ever they reveal their secret power they are doomed to instant death.' But the shepherd persisted in his demand until, seeing that the king would not give in, he turned to go.

But the king stopped him, saying, 'O you who have saved my son, seeing you are determined to have this wish and no other, I shall no longer refuse you. Open your mouth.'

The shepherd obeyed and the king blew three times into his mouth with a fiery breath. Then the king bade him blow back into his mouth. This the shepherd did and the king said, 'Now the language of animals is yours, but remember, never share your secret with anyone or you will die instantly. Farewell.'

The shepherd left the snake palace and as he returned through the enchanted forest he found he could understand every word that passed between birds, rabbits, squirrels, foxes and all the other creatures.

At last he came to the glade where he had left his flock and in wonderment found that they were all there. He was just settling down to rest on the soft moss when two ravens alighted on a nearby tree and began to gossip. Said one of them, 'If this man only knew that under the moss where he is resting lies a cave full of silver and gold, he would hurry off to get himself a cart and spade.' At this the shepherd leapt up, gathered his flock and hurried home to tell his master, a wealthy farmer.

The farmer was an honest, generous man and though he helped the shepherd dig until they came to a cave brimful of gold and silver coins, he refused to accept a single piece, saying, 'It was you that God

45

gave it to. Build yourself a house, marry and start your own farm and may fortune bless you.'

The shepherd followed his master's advice and so well did his farm flourish that he soon became the richest man in the district. He was so rich in fact that the local squire was glad to accept him as a son-in-law. His young wife was beautiful, but very headstrong. At first the simple shepherd was too impressed by her superior education to notice her faults. Although he was now a wealthy man, he never forgot his humble origin and one day before Christmas he told his wife: 'Make ready enough food and wine for a hundred men. Tomorrow we will go to our farm and feast the servants while I myself guard the sheep.'

So one bitter winter night when the snow lay thick on the ground the kind man went to watch over the sheep while his shepherds feasted and made merry round a roaring fire. Just before midnight the wolves began to howl and the dogs to growl. Then the shepherd heard the leader of the wolf pack asking the dogs in their own tongue: 'Can we come and kill the sheep, and then we can all feast on them together?' To this the dogs answered, 'With pleasure, for we are sick of guarding other people's property.' Only one old dog, with but two fangs left in his head, snarled at them; 'The devil take you: as long as I have these two fangs left, you shall not touch my master's sheep.'

Next morning the shepherd ordered his servants

to kill all his dogs except the one faithful old hound. The servants pleaded with him, saying that he was surely mad to kill a whole pack of well-trained sheep-dogs. But their master insisted that they carry out his orders. Then he mounted a piebald horse and his wife rode on a grey mare, and they set off for home. Soon the mare began to lag behind, whereupon the horse neighed, 'Hurry up! Why do you dawdle?' To which the mare replied, 'It is easy for you to say "Hurry". You have only the master on your back but I carry the mistress, whose rules are a burden to the whole household.' Hearing these words, the shepherd burst into such a hearty laugh that his wife spurred on her mare to ask him the cause of his mirth.

He was unable to explain and this only made her the more inquisitive, till at last, worn out by her obstinate questioning, he tried to excuse himself by saying, 'Don't keep asking me, for if I tell you the reason I shall die forthwith.'

But his wife was a stubborn creature, and thought he was joking again, and continued to press him for an answer, until, poor man, he could stand it no longer, being quite unable to withstand her nagging. So when he reached home he sadly ordered a coffin to be made and placed in the courtyard. Then he stepped into it and told his wife, 'I'm going to lie in this coffin, for I shall die as soon as I tell you why I laughed.'

But before lying down in the coffin he turned to

47

take one last look at his beloved fields, and he saw his faithful old dog come running towards him. Seeing what was about to become of his master, the poor hound began to howl woefully and refused to touch the delicious cakes his mistress offered him. The cock, however, came strutting in from the yard, eager to seize any morsel that happened to be lying about. The dog began to rebuke him for his heartlessness, saying: 'You greedy creature, how can you think of nothing but food when our poor master is about to die?' But the cock only tossed his crimson comb and answered, 'What do I care if such a fool is about to die! Why, I have a hundred wives and I gather them all around a grain of corn, only to gobble it up myself when they are all assembled. And if any of them dares to protest I just peck them. But he, the fool, cannot control his one and only spouse.'

Hearing this, the shepherd leaped from the coffin, seized a stick and called to his wife: 'Just listen, my good woman. If you still insist on knowing why I laughed, I shall beat the living daylights out of you.'

Needless to say his wife instantly stopped her nagging and what's more, she never nagged again and they lived happily ever after.

# The Wicked Little Jackal

Africa, as you probably know, is always a very hot country, but in the year when this story took place it was *exceptionally* hot. There was no rain, all the rivers and pools dried up, the grass withered and the trees died. The animals went around with their tongues hanging out, dying of thirst, waiting and waiting for the rain to fall.

At long last it did fall. The grass grew green once more, the trees stood up straight and the animals quenched their thirst in the newly filled pools and rivers.

A meeting of all the animals was called to decide what to do if another terrible drought were to come. After a lot of discussion they all agreed that the best plan was to dig a very large, very deep hole near a spring so that the water could trickle into it and build up into a great pool. Then they wouldn't have to worry if no rain fell, because there would always be water in the pool.

'Who is going to dig this hole?' asked the elephant.

'You, my friend,' replied the lion, who, as king of

49

the forest, was in charge of the meeting. 'And you, and you, and you, and you, and you,' the lion continued, pointing to each animal in turn. 'We are *all* going to dig this hole, because we shall *all* be drinking the water in it. I, of course, will supervise the proceedings.'

He paused and looked round sternly. 'I take it that you all agree to do a share of the digging?' The animals said, 'Oh yes, Your Majesty, we all agree to do our share of the digging.'

So they went and found a spring and not far from it they all began to dig. Did I say 'all'? Well, not exactly all, because the jackal did not join in. Now, everybody knew the jackal was mean and greedy and always stealing other people's food instead of hunting for his own. Oh yes, they all knew Brother Jackal very well. But they did expect him to help with the digging.

'Come on, Jackal,' they all urged, 'come and give a hand. You'll be using this water as well, you know.'

But the jackal just sat and laughed. 'Work?' he said. 'Not likely. You work and I will enjoy the water when you have finished.'

The animals were very angry but they knew it was not much use arguing with the cunning little jackal, so they went on working while the jackal just sat and laughed.

At long last the pool was finished and the beautiful, fresh spring water began to flow into it.

'And now,' said the lion, 'we must build a high

wall round it, just leaving room enough for a narrow gate. And then we will appoint a guard to watch over it so that the jackal won't be able to come and steal the water from the pool which we have all worked so hard to build. I am determined to see that he shall not enjoy the fruits of our labours.'

So they built the wall and made a strong little gate.

'Now,' said the lion, 'who will volunteer to guard the gate?'

'I will, Your Majesty, I will,' cried the hare.

'Excellent,' said the lion. 'I think Hare will make a very good guard – he has first-class eyesight, he can see in the dark and he is, of course, one of the fastest creatures in the whole animal kingdom.'

That night, as the hare sat and watched, the jackal came strolling past, nibbling a piece of honeycomb. The cunning thing pretended not to see the hare (though, of course, he *had* seen him) and walked past again, still nibbling. 'Delicious honey, this,' he remarked, as though talking to himself. 'So sweet, so succulent!' The hare felt very tempted. 'Is it really so very tasty?' he asked. The jackal pretended not to hear but continued to nibble and say the most tantalizing things. The hare asked once more: 'Is the honeycomb really so wonderfully succulent?'

'Oh, is that you, Hare?' asked the cunning jackal. 'I hadn't noticed you in the dark. Yes, indeed. It's the most wonderful honeycomb I have ever tasted, and I'm quite an expert in these matters. Of course, I would gladly let you have a taste of it but all those angry animals would come and attack me if I dared come near you. You are supposed to be guarding this water, I understand.'

'I promise you won't come to any harm,' said the hare.

'Well, just to be on the safe side,' said the jackal, 'let me tie your paws and I'll put some honey into your mouth.'

The hare agreed, for he thought that the jackal didn't really want any water. So the jackal tied the hare's paws, then jumped right over him, splash! into the cool, clear pool. He drank and drank to his heart's content. Then he stirred up the mud at the bottom of the pool to make it look as messy as possible and ran off without giving the hare any taste of the honey at all.

You can imagine how cross the animals were when they found their beautiful pool, at which they had worked so hard, all muddy and dirty. They started arguing and quarrelling among themselves about who should be the next to keep guard over the pool. And poor old Hare felt very foolish, sitting there with his paws tied up.

At last, when there was a lull in all the squabbling, the tortoise spoke up. 'I will guard the water,' she said. They were all taken aback for a moment, the tortoise being usually such a quiet creature, but eventually they agreed.

So that night the tortoise, with her head tucked

into her shell and her feet and tail well drawn in, sat by the gate and waited.

Presently the jackal came along, nibbling at his honeycomb and chatting to himself.

'How would you like to taste some of my delicious honey?' he asked the tortoise. But the tortoise kept perfectly still and made no reply whatsoever.

The jackal tried again. 'It's the most delicious honey in the whole world. Do have some.'

But the tortoise remained perfectly motionless. The jackal took a closer look but he couldn't seem to make up his mind which was the tail and which was the head.

'She must be asleep,' he muttered. 'I'll go and help myself to a drink in the pool.' And he was just about to step over the tortoise when crack! out popped the tortoise's little head and she caught the jackal by the hind leg. The jackal screeched and kicked and howled but the tortoise would not let go. He offered to give her all his honey and to get her any juicy green leaves she might fancy, but the tortoise held on and would not let go.

At last, with the first rays of dawn, the animals came along to see how everything had been going on and to have a drink in their pool.

When they saw the jackal trapped by his leg in the tortoise's mouth, they thought it such a comical sight that they roared with laughter. The jackal simply hated being laughed at and he felt most embarrassed at being found in that humiliating position. He was,

after all, supposed to be a most cunning animal. As they all sat there, quite helpless with laughter, he just couldn't bear it any longer and gave one last desperate kick. The tortoise, feeling a bit sorry for him, let go, and the jackal ran away as fast as his legs could carry him. He ran and ran and ran. And never, ever again did he come back to spoil the animals' beautiful pool.

And all the animals were very grateful to the tortoise and treated her with great honour.

# Puss and Pup

Once upon a time Puss and Pup kept house together.
They had their own little cottage in the wood. Here
they lived together and tried to do everything just
like real grown-up people. But somehow they
couldn't always manage this. You see, they had small
clumsy paws, without any fingers like people have,
only little soft pads with claws on them. So they
couldn't do everything just like real grown-ups. And
they didn't go to school, because school is not meant
for animals.

Of course it isn't. School is only for children.

Their home was not always as tidy as it might have
been. Some things they did well, and others not so
well. And sometimes there was rather a mess.

One day they noticed that the cottage floor was
very dirty.

'I say, Pup,' said Puss, 'our floor's horribly dirty.
Don't you think so?'

'Yes, I do. It really is rather dirty,' said Pup. 'Just
look how grubby it's made my paws.'

'They're filthy,' said Puss. 'Ugh, you ought to be

ashamed of yourself! We must scrub the floor. People don't have dirty floors. They scrub them.'

'All right,' replied Pup. 'But how are we going to do it?'

'Oh, it's easy,' said Puss. 'You go and fetch some water, and I'll see to the rest.'

Pup took a pail and went for water. Meanwhile Puss took a piece of soap out of her bag and put it on the table. Then she went off to the box-room for something; I expect she kept a piece of smoked mouse there.

While she was away Pup came back with the water and saw something lying on the table. He unwrapped it. It was pink.

'Ha, ha! This looks good,' said Pup to himself. And because it made him feel hungry, he pushed the whole piece into his mouth and started chewing it.

But it didn't taste so good. Soon Puss came in and heard Pup making all sorts of funny spluttering noises. She saw that Pup's mouth was full of foam and his eyes were streaming with tears.

'Goodness me!' cried Puss. 'Whatever's happened to you, Pup? You must be ill. There's foam dripping from your mouth. Whatever's the matter?'

'Well,' said Pup, 'I found something lying on the table. I thought it might be some cheese, or a piece of cake, so I ate it. But it stings horribly and makes my mouth all full of foam.'

'What a silly you are!' scolded Puss. 'That was soap! Soap's for washing with, not eating.'

'Oh,' said Pup. 'So that's why it hurts so much. Ow, ow, it stings, ow, it stings!'

'Have a good drink of water,' suggested Puss; 'that'll stop it smarting.'

Pup drank away until he had finished up all the water. His mouth had stopped smarting by now, but there was still plenty of foam. So he went and wiped his muzzle on the grass outside. Then he had to go and fetch some more water because he had drunk it all and there was none left. Luckily Puss had some money, and she went off to buy some more soap.

'I won't eat that again,' said Pup, when Puss returned with the soap. 'But, Puss, how are we going to manage without a scrubbing brush?'

'I've already thought about that,' said Puss. 'You've got a rough, bristly coat, just like a brush. We can scrub the floor with you.'

'Right ho!' said Pup. And Puss took the soap and the pail of water, and knelt down on the floor. Then she scrubbed the whole floor with Pup.

By now the floor was all wet, and it wasn't any too clean either.

'We ought to rub it over with something dry,' said Puss.

'I'll tell you what,' said Pup. 'I'm sopping wet, but you're dry, and your fur is nice and soft. It'll make a lovely floorcloth. I'll dry the floor with you.'

So he took hold of Puss and dried the whole floor with her.

The floor was now washed and dried, but Puss and Pup were all wet and terribly dirty from having been used to wash the floor.

'Well, we do look a sight!' they both said, looking at each other. 'We've got the floor clean all right, but now look at us! We can't possibly stay like this. Everybody will laugh. We'll have to be sent to the wash.'

'Let's wash each other, like they do at the laundry,' said Pup. 'You wash me, and when I'm done, I'll wash you.'

'Very well,' said Puss.

They filled the tub of water and took a scrubbing-board. Pup got into the tub and Puss washed him. She rubbed him so much on the scrubbing-board that Pup begged her not to press so hard, as his legs were getting all tangled up.

When Pup was finished, Puss got into the tub and Pup scrubbed and squeezed her so much that she begged him not to press her so hard on the scrubbing-board in case he made a hole in her fur.

Then they wrung each other out.

'Now we'll hang ourselves out to dry,' said Puss. So they put out the clothes-line.

'First I'll hang you up on the line, and when you're

up, you can get down and hang me up,' Pup told Puss.

So Pup took hold of Puss and hung her up, just like washing. They didn't need any pegs, because they could hold on to the line with their claws. Once Puss was on the line, she jumped down and hung up Pup.

By now the two of them were hanging nicely and the sun was shining brightly.

'The sun's shining on us,' cried Pup. 'We'll soon be dry.' No sooner had he said this than it began to rain.

'Oh, dear, it's raining!' shouted Puss and Pup. 'The washing will get wet. Let's take it down!'

They jumped down quickly and ran to the cottage for shelter.

'Is it still raining?' asked Puss.

'It's stopped,' said Pup, and sure enough the sun was out again.

'Let's hang the washing out again, then,' said Puss.

So they hung themselves on the line a second time. First Pup put Puss up, and as soon as she was hanging up she jumped down and put up Pup. So they both hung on the line, just like washing, and were very pleased at the way the sun shone and made such a good drying day. But then it began to rain again.

'It's raining! Our washing will get wet!' cried Puss and Pup. And they ran for shelter. Soon the sun came out again, and again they hung each other up on the clothes-line. Then it started raining, and off they scampered. Then the sun came out again and they hung themselves up again, and so it went on till the evening. By that time they were both quite dry.

'Our washing's dry,' they said. 'Let's put it in the basket.'

So they clambered into the basket. But then they felt so sleepy that they both fell asleep. And they slept in the basket right through until the next morning.

# Can Men Be Such Fools
As All That?

I was nurse to the little Duke of Chinon, who lived in the great grim castle on the hill above the town where the Rag-picker's Son lived. The little Duke, of course, had everything that the poor boy hadn't: fine clothes to wear, white bread and chicken to eat, and a pedigree spaniel called Hubert for a playfellow.

Except for all these differences, the two boys were as like as two peas; when I took the little Duke walking by the river, and we happened to meet the Rag-picker's Son, you could not have told one from the other, if one hadn't worn satin and the other rags, while one had a dirty face and hands and the other was as clean as a new pin. Everybody remarked on it.

The little Duke used to look longingly at the poor boy, though, for he was allowed to splash about in the water of the river as he pleased; and the water of the Loire is more beautiful to splash about in than any water in France, for it is as clear as honey, and has the brightest gold sand-bed you can imagine; and when you get out of the town, it runs between sandy shores, where green willows grow, and flowers of all sorts. But it was against my orders to let the little Duke play in the water, and I had to obey them, though I was sorry for him; for I knew what boys like.

One day as we were out walking, the Duke's spaniel, Hubert, ran up to the Rag-picker's Son's mongrel, Jacques, and they touched noses and made friends. And the Duke and the poor boy smiled at each other and said, 'Hullo!' After that, when we met, the boys always nodded, or winked, or made some sign of friendship; and one day the Rag-picker's Son jerked his thumb at the river, as much as to say, 'Come in and play with me!'

The Duke looked at me, and I shook my head, so the Duke shook his. But he was cross with me for the rest of the day.

The next day I missed him, and there was a great hullabaloo all over the castle. I and his guardian and all his attendants went down to the town to find him; and asked everybody we met if they had seen him; and presently we met the Rag-picker, who said, 'Yes, I saw him an hour ago, going along the river-bank with my son.' And we all ran along the bank, the Rag-picker too, and most of the townsfolk behind us.

A mile along the bank, there they were, the two boys, standing in the middle of the river as bare as when they were born, splashing about and screaming

with laughter, and on the shore lay a little heap of
clothes, rags and fine linen all thrown down anyhow
together. We were all very angry with the boys, and
called and shouted to them to come out of the water;
and they shouted back that they wouldn't. At last
the Rag-picker waded in and fetched them out by
the scruffs of their necks. And there they stood before
us, naked and grinning and full of fun, and just as
the Duke's guardian was going to scold his charge,
and the Rag-picker to scold his son, they suddenly
found themselves in a pickle! For without their
clothes, washed clean by the river, they were so
exactly alike that we didn't know which was which.
And the boys saw that we didn't and grinned more
than ever.

'Now then, my boy!' said the Rag-picker to one of
them. But the boy he spoke to did not answer, for
he knew if he talked it would give the game away.

And the Duke's guardian said to the other boy,
'Come, monseigneur!' But that boy too shook his
head and kept mum.

Then I had a bright idea, and said to the boys, 'Put
on your clothes!' for I thought that would settle it.
But the two boys picked up the clothes as they came:
one of them put on the ragged shirt and the satin
coat, and the other put on the fine shirt and the
ragged coat. So we were no better off than before.

Then the Rag-picker and the Duke's guardian lost
their tempers, and raised their sticks and gave each
of the boys three strokes, thinking that might help;

but all it did was to make them squeal, and when a
boy squeals it doesn't matter if he's a Duke or a
beggar, the sound is just the same.

'This is dreadful,' said the Duke's guardian; 'for all we know, we shall get the boys mixed for ever, and I shall take the Rag-picker's Son back to the castle, and the Duke will grow up as the Rag-picker's Son. Is there no way of telling which is which? Can we all be such fools as that?'

Just as we were scratching our heads and cudgelling our brains, and wondering what on earth to do next there came a sound of yelps and barks; and out of the willows ran Jacques and Hubert, who had been off on their own, playing together. They came racing towards us joyously, and straight as a die Jacques jumped up and licked the face of the boy in the satin coat, while Hubert licked the boy in the ragged jacket.

So then there was no doubt about it. We made the boys change their coats, and the Rag-picker marched his son home to bed, and the guardian did the same with the Duke. And that night the Duke and the poor boy had exactly the same supper to go to sleep on; in other words, nothing and plenty of it.

But how had the dogs known in the twink of an eye what we hadn't known at all? Can men be such fools as all that?

# The Little Hare and the Tiger

Everyone in the forest was afraid of the extremely fierce tiger who, every day without fail, would come on his regular prowl and carry off not just one animal or two, but three or four or even more. For he was a very greedy tiger. No one could ever feel safe, for no one knew who was to be the next victim.

One day the jackal had a bright idea. He called a meeting of the animals and spoke to them in the following terms.

'Fellow animals,' he began. 'I would like to suggest that we undertake to send the tiger one animal regularly every day for his dinner. You know how fat and lazy he is getting. So if he gets his regular daily feast guaranteed by us, he won't have to come stalking through the forest killing everyone he meets.' Now the jackal was very cunning. He was thinking to himself, 'We'll send all the *smaller* animals to the tiger first and then I'll be safe for a long time to come.'

The tiger himself thought this was an excellent plan and all the other animals agreed too – all, that is, except the little hare. When he heard that he was

66

to be first to be the tiger's dinner, he wasn't at all pleased. Not surprising, of course. So the little hare spoke up and said, 'No, I'm not going. No, no, no, a thousand times no.'

This got the animals very worried indeed. They were afraid that if they kept the tiger waiting, he would come stalking along in his usual manner and carry off several of them. But try as they might they simply could not persuade the little hare. He just sat, with a thoughtful look on his face, muttering, 'No, no, no.' In the distance they could hear the tiger roaring impatiently. Luckily he thought his dinner was on the way and he felt too lazy to come and fetch it himself. Suddenly, the little hare, who had been growing more and more thoughtful, sprang up and shouted, 'I'm off,' and off he ran, as fast as lightning, or maybe even a little faster.

The other animals gave a sigh of relief because they thought the little hare had at last been persuaded to go to the tiger, and present himself as the first dinner. Nothing of the kind, of course. But mind you, he did go to the tiger's cave, right inside, too, but just outside the reach of the tiger's paws.

The tiger, very lazy, had been having a little grumbling sort of snooze. When he saw the little hare, he growled, 'Come here, you pathetic little creature. You're late enough already.'

The little hare burst into tears. 'I'm so sorry, Tiger, to be so thin and be such a poor dinner for you. My brother was so beautifully fat.'

'Your brother!' roared the tiger. 'Your fat brother, you say? Then why didn't *he* come, instead of you?' And this made him angrier and hungrier than ever.

'Well, he did, actually,' sobbed the little hare. 'That is, he did start out to get here, but they unfortunately got him on the way. Boo, hoo!' and he gave a loud wail.

'Who got him?' roared the tiger, so loudly that the ceiling of the cave nearly burst.

'The other tiger,' sobbed the little hare. 'You know, the one who lives in that hole in the bushes.'

'Lead me to him,' thundered the tiger. 'I'll teach him to eat up all the fat hares and leave the skinny little ones like you.'

'Very well,' said the little hare, 'come this way, Tiger, and I will lead you to his den.'

The tiger, like all other cats, could not see too well in the bright sunlight and he peered about suspiciously as he followed the little hare through the tall jungle grass. All of a sudden, without any warning whatsoever, the little hare darted off into some bushes. 'This way, Tiger,' he called out. And the great beast followed him and found himself in an open space by the side of a deep hole, or what looked like a deep hole. 'This is the other tiger's den,' said the little hare in a very scared voice. 'The one that ate my fat brother.'

The tiger went up to the very edge of the hole and leaned over. Looking up at him was the face of the most ferocious tiger he had ever seen.

'Grrrrrr . . . ' roared the tiger. 'I'm going to teach you a lesson you will never forget,' and he jumped and – splash! Down and down he went, for the hole was a deep, deep well filled with shining water, clear as a looking-glass, and the tiger looking up at him had really been his own greedy self. And so that was the end of *him*. For he never, ever got out of that well again.

And as for the little hare, he went back and told all the other animals that they had nothing more to fear from the greedy tiger. And he was acclaimed the most heroic little hare in the whole forest.

# Six Foolish Fishermen

Alf, Bill, Clem, Dick, Ed and Fred were six brothers who were all very keen fishermen.

One fine morning they decided to go down to the river to see who could catch the most fish.

Alf said he would fish from his boat, Bill from a raft, Clem from a bridge over the river, Dick from a tree overhanging the river, and Ed from a little island in the middle of the river. Fred said:

'I shall walk along the bank of the river and fish.'

They fished all through that sunny morning, they all caught lots of fish and they were all very pleased with themselves.

But Alf was worried about one thing, one rather important thing. As all the brothers had been fishing in different places he wondered whether they were all safe and sound. 'Perhaps Clem has fallen off the bridge and got drowned,' he thought. 'Or maybe Dick has slipped off that tree-trunk. I had better count all us brothers to see if we are all here,' and he started to count: 'There's Bill on the raft, that makes one. There's Clem on the bridge, that's two.

I can see Dick on the tree, that's three. There's Ed on the island, that's four. And Fred on the bank, that's five. But we are six. Good gracious me! One brother has been lost.' He was so upset, he forgot to count himself.

Bill, on the raft, heard him. 'Have we really lost one?' he asked and he too began to count.

'There's Clem on the bridge. That makes one. Dick is on the tree. That's two. I spy Ed on the island. That's three. And there's Fred on the bank, that's four. Oh yes, of course, that's Alf looking worried in the boat, that's five. Five! Where's the sixth? Oh dear, we've lost one.'

Clem spotted him from the bridge. 'I'm going to have a re-count,' he said. 'There's Dick on that branch, that's one. Ed is quite visible on the island, that's two. Fred is on the bank, that's three. Alf is still there in his boat, that's four, and Bill is floating towards me on his raft, making five. Oh goodness me! Only five! We have indeed lost one.'

He was so upset that Dick counted them again just to make sure, but he too only found five. And Ed and Fred weren't any luckier either when they checked.

So they all left the spots from where they had been fishing and ran up and down the river-bank trying to find the body of their unfortunate drowned brother.

Just then a boy came strolling along the bank with his fishing-line and an empty basket. He too had been fishing but had not caught a single thing.

'Why do you all look so worried?' he asked the

brothers. 'You all seem to have had a very good morning's fishing.'

'Because one of our brothers has been drowned,' they explained in great distress. 'There were six of us when we started out, and now there are only five.'

The boy made a quick count and saw there *were* six brothers.

'Look,' he said, 'I can help you find your lost brother. When I tickle each of you on the neck, I want you to count.' He went up to Alf and tickled him. 'One!' cried Alf, laughing. Then he went up to Bill and tickled *his* neck. 'Two!' cried Bill. And 'Three!' shouted Clem. And 'Four!' laughed Dick. And 'Five!' chuckled Ed. And 'Six!' shrieked Fred.

And 'Six!' all the brothers roared in unison, realizing they were all safe and sound. They all embraced one another and shouted for joy. And in gratitude to the boy they gave him all the fish they had caught.

# The Ugsome Thing

There was once a monster called the Ugsome Thing. He was round and fat and scaly and he had long teeth twisted like sticks of barley sugar. He lived in a castle and had many servants to wait on him. They had to clean his castle and cook his food and till his fields and tend his flocks and herds. Though they worked hard, he never paid them a penny in wages.

The Ugsome Thing had a magic power, and if he could make anyone lose his temper, that person became his slave and had to obey him.

At this time, the Ugsome Thing had all the servants he wanted except for one – he had not a good washer-woman. His clothes were often dirty and badly ironed. Now, as he went through the village near his castle, he passed a cottage garden which was full, on a Monday, of the whitest clothes he had ever seen. They were like snow, blowing and billowing on the line stretched between two apple trees. He decided to make the old woman who lived there come and do his washing. It would be very simple. He only had to make her lose her temper and she would be in his power.

So one Monday morning, when her clothes-line was full of the whitest wash possible, he cut the line with his knife and the snowy clothes lay tumbled on the dirty grass. Surely that would make her lose her temper.

When the old woman saw what had happened, she came running out of the door, and instead of losing her temper she said quietly:

'Well! Well! Well! The chimney has been smoking this morning and I'm sure some smuts must have blown on my washing. Anyway, it will be a good idea to wash it again. How lucky that the line broke just this morning and no other!'

So she picked up armfuls of the dirty clothes and went back to the wash-house, singing as she went.

The Ugsome Thing was very angry and he gnashed his barley-sugar teeth, but he soon thought of another idea to make her lose her temper.

On Tuesday the Ugsome Thing visited the old woman again. He saw that she had milked her cow, Daisy, and that the milk stood in a pan in the dairy. He turned the whole pan of milk sour. Surely that would make her lose her temper.

When the old woman saw the pan of sour milk she said:

'Well! Well! Well! Now I shall have to make it into cream cheese and that will be a treat for my grandchildren when they come to tea. They love having cream cheese on their scones. How lucky the milk turned sour just today and no other!'

The Ugsome Thing was very angry and he gnashed his barley-sugar teeth, but he soon thought of another idea to make her lose her temper.

On Wednesday the Ugsome Thing visited the old woman again. He turned all the hollyhocks in her garden into thistles, the red ones and the pink ones and the double yellow ones. She was very proud of her garden. Surely that would make her lose her temper.

'Well! Well! Well!' said the old woman when she saw thistles growing by the wall instead of hollyhocks. 'I was going to pick a bunch of hollyhocks today for my friend's birthday, but now I shall make her a pin-cushion instead, and stuff it with thistledown.'

So she made a velvet pin-cushion and stuffed it with thistledown and embroidered a flower on it. It looked nearly as pretty as the hollyhocks and lasted much longer.

'How lucky I am that I noticed all those thistles just today and no other,' she said, as she sewed up the pin-cushion.

The Ugsome Thing was very angry and gnashed his barley-sugar teeth, but he soon thought of another idea to make her lose her temper.

On Thursday the Ugsome Thing stretched a piece of string across the stairs, hoping that the old woman

would trip over it and fall. Surely that would make her lose her temper.

The old woman did fall, and hurt her knee, and had to hop on one leg to the shed to milk Daisy the cow.

'Well! Well! Well!' said the old woman. 'I can't do any housework today. I shall lie on the sofa and get on with my patchwork quilt. What a nice change that will be! I may even get it finished. How lucky I am that I tripped over just today, and no other!'

The Ugsome Thing was very angry and gnashed his barley-sugar teeth, but he soon thought of another idea to make her lose her temper.

On Friday the Ugsome Thing visited the old woman again. He saw her going to the hen-house to collect the eggs. She had three white hens and they had each laid an egg. As she was walking past the apple tree, he flipped a branch in her face and she dropped the bowl and broke the eggs. Surely that would make her lose her temper.

'Well! Well! Well!' said the old woman. 'Now I shall have to have scrambled eggs for dinner and supper, and scrambled eggs are my favourite food. How lucky I am that the eggs broke just today and no other!'

Now the Ugsome Thing was very angry indeed and he gnashed his barley-sugar teeth, but he soon thought of another idea to make her lose her temper. This idea was a very nasty one, because he was very, very angry indeed.

On Saturday the Ugsome Thing set the old woman's cottage on fire. Surely that would make her lose her temper. The flames shot up the walls and soon the thatched roof caught fire.

'Well! Well! Well!' said the old woman. 'That's the last of my old cottage. I was fond of it, but it was falling to pieces and the roof let in the rain and there were holes in the floor.'

When the Ugsome Thing came along to see if the old woman had lost her temper, he found her busy baking potatoes in the hot ashes, and handing them round to the village children.

'Have a potato?' she said to the Ugsome Thing, holding one out on the point of a stick.

It smelled so good that the Ugsome Thing took it and crammed it into his mouth whole, because he was very greedy, and some of it went down the wrong way. He choked so hard with rage and hot potato that he burst like a balloon and there was nothing left but a piece of shrivelled, scaly, greenish skin. A little boy threw it on the fire, thinking it was an old rag, and it burned with a spluttering yellow flame.

By this time, most of the people in the village were lining up to have a baked potato, and while they waited they planned how they could help the old woman.

'I'll build the walls of a new cottage,' said one.

'I'll make the roof,' said another.

'I'll put in the windows,' said a third.

'I'll paper the walls,' said a fourth.

'We'll give her a carpet – sheets – a blanket – a kettle – ' said the women. By the time all the potatoes were cooked and eaten, her friends had promised the old woman all she needed for a new cottage.

The new cottage was not old and tumbledown like the first one, but dry and comfortable with a sunny porch. Daisy had a new shed and the dog a new kennel. Only the cat was disappointed as there were no mice for her to chase. There were no holes for the mice to live in.

# The Woman Who Always Argued

Once upon a time, there was an old man and an old woman. The man was all right. It was the woman who was the trouble.

Whatever anyone said, she said the opposite. If the fishmonger said, 'I've some good herrings today,' she said, 'No, I want sprats.' If the butcher said, 'I've got lamb chops today,' she said, 'No, I want beef.' If anyone opened a window, she shut it. If someone shut it, she opened it. She vowed that hens were ducks, and cats were dogs, and when it was raining she said it was snowing.

As for her poor old husband, what trouble he had. He was with her all the time, you see, because they did the farming together. So you can imagine he was very tired of it.

One morning they went across the bridge to look at their cornfield.

'Ah,' said the man. 'The corn will be ready by Tuesday.'

'Monday,' said the woman.

'Very well then, Monday,' said the man. 'I'll get John and Eric to help harvest it.'

'No you won't,' said the woman. 'You'll get James and Robert.'

'All right,' said the man. 'James and Robert. We'll start at seven.'

'At six,' said his wife.

'At six,' agreed the man. 'The weather will be good for it.'

'It will be bad,' she said. 'It will pour.'

'Well, whether it rains or shines,' said the man, getting fed up, 'whether we do it Monday at seven or Tuesday at six, we'll cut it with scythes.'

'Shears,' said his wife.

'Shears?' said the man, amazed. 'Cut the corn with shears? What are you talking about! We'll cut with scythes!' (For with shears, you see, you have to bend down and go snip, snip, at one tiny bit after another. But with the lovely curved scythe, you go *swoosh!* and half the corn falls down flat.) 'We'll cut with scythes!' said the man.

'Shears!' said the woman.

They went over the bridge, still arguing.

'Scythes!' said the man.

'Shears!' said the woman.

So angry was the woman that the man was arguing back that she didn't look where she was going, and she fell off the bridge into the water. When she bobbed up again, you'd think she'd shout 'Help!' but not her. She shouted 'Shears!' and the man only just had time to shout 'Scythes!' before she bobbed back again.

Up she came again, and 'Shears!' she shouted. The man yelled back 'Scythes!' and she disappeared again. She came up again once more, and this time there was so much water in her mouth, because she would keep opening it to argue, that she couldn't say anything at all, so as her head went back again she stuck out her hand and with the fingers she silently went snip-snip, like shears above the water, snip-snip. Then she was gone.

'Stupid old woman!' said the man, stamping his foot. 'Stupid, obstinate, argumentative old woman!'

He went to the village to get his friends to help him find her. They all came back to the bridge, and searched in the water. But she wasn't there.

'If the water has carried her away,' said one of them, 'she will be downstream. That is the way the river flows, and everything in the water must go with the river.'

So they went downstream and looked, but they couldn't find her.

Suddenly the old man shouted. 'What a fool I am! Everything else in the water would go with the river, it's true. But not my wife! She's bound to do the opposite. She'll be floating the other way, mark my words!'

So they ran up the stream, and sure enough, there she was, the opposite way to everything else. And

what do you know, she was insisting on floating right *up* the waterfall!

# The Magician's Heart

We all have our weaknesses. Mine is mulberries.
Yours, perhaps, motor-cars. Professor Taykin's was
christenings – royal christenings. He always expected
to be asked to the christening parties of all the little
royal babies, and of course he never was, because he
was not a lord, or a duke, or a seller of bacon and
tea, or anything really high class, but merely a wicked
magician, who by economy and strict attention to
customers had worked up a very good business of
his own. He had not always been wicked. He was
born quite good, I believe, and his old nurse, who
had long since married a farmer and retired into the
calm of country life, always used to say that he was
the duckiest little boy in a plaid frock with the dearest
little fat legs. But he had changed since he was a boy,
as a good many other people do – perhaps it was his
trade. I dare say you've noticed that cobblers are
usually thin, and brewers are generally fat, and
magicians are almost always wicked.

Well, his weakness (for christenings) grew stronger
and stronger because it was never indulged, and at

last he 'took the bull into his own hands', as the Irish footman at the palace said, and went to a christening without being asked. It was a very grand party given by the King of the Fortunate Islands, and the little Prince was christened Fortunatus. No one took any notice of Professor Taykin. They were too polite to turn him out, but they made him wish he'd never come. He felt quite an outsider, as indeed he was, and this made him furious. So that when all the bright, light, laughing fairy godmothers were crowding round the blue satin cradle, and giving gifts of beauty and strength and goodness to the baby, the Magician suddenly did a very difficult charm (in his head, like you do mental arithmetic), and said:

'Young Forty may be all that, but I say he shall be the stupidest prince in the world,' and on that he vanished in a puff of red smoke with a smell like the Fifth of November in a back garden on Streatham Hill, and as he left no address the King of the Fortunate Islands couldn't prosecute him for high treason.

Taykin was very glad to think that he had made such a lot of people unhappy – the whole court was in tears when he left, including the baby – and he looked in the papers for another royal christening, so that he could go to that and make a lot more people miserable. And there was one fixed for the very next Wednesday. The Magician went to that too, disguised as a wealthy merchant.

This time the baby was a girl. Taykin kept close to the pink velvet cradle, and when all the nice qualities

87

in the world had been given to the Princess he suddenly said: 'Little Aura may be all that, but I say she shall be the ugliest princess in all the world.'

And instantly she was. It was terrible. And she had been such a beautiful baby too. Everyone had been saying that she was the most beautiful baby they had ever seen. This sort of thing is often said at christenings.

Having uglified the unfortunate little Princess the Magician did the spell (in his mind, just as you do your spelling) to make himself vanish, but to his horror there was no red smoke and no smell of fireworks, and there he was, still, where he now very much wished not to be. Because one of the fairies there had seen, just one second too late to save the Princess, what he was up to, and had made a strong little charm in a great hurry to prevent his vanishing. This fairy was a White Witch, and of course you know that White Magic is much stronger than Black Magic, as well as more suited for drawing-room performances. So there the Magician stood, 'looking like a thunder-struck pig,' as someone unkindly said, and the dear White Witch bent down and kissed the baby Princess.

'There!' she said, 'you can keep that kiss till you want it. When the time comes you'll know what to do with it. The Magician can't vanish, sire. You'd better arrest him.'

'Arrest that person,' said the King, pointing to

Taykin. 'I suppose your charms are of a permanent nature, madam.'

'Quite,' said the Fairy, 'at least they never go till there's no longer any use for them.'

So the Magician was shut up in an enormously high tower, and allowed to play with magic; but none

89

of his spells could act outside the tower so he was never able to pass the extra double guard that watched outside night and day. The King would have liked to have the Magician executed but the White Witch warned him that this would never do.

'Don't you see,' she said, 'he's the only person who can make the Princess beautiful again. And he'll do it some day. But don't you go asking him to do it. He'll never do anything to oblige you. He's that sort of man.'

So the years rolled on. The Magician stayed in the tower and did magic and was very bored, for it is dull to take white rabbits out of your hat, and your hat out of nothing, when there's no one to see you.

Prince Fortunatus was such a stupid little boy that he got lost quite early in the story, and went about the country saying his name was James, which it wasn't. A baker's wife found him and adopted him, and sold the diamond buttons of his little overcoat for three hundred pounds, and as she was a very honest woman she put two hundred away for James to have when he grew up.

The years rolled on. Aura continued to be hideous, and she was very unhappy, till on her twentieth birthday her married cousin Belinda came to see her. Now Belinda had been made ugly in her cradle too, so she could sympathize as no one else could.

'But I got out of it all right, and so will you,' said Belinda. 'I'm sure the first thing to do is to find a magician.'

'Father banished them all twenty years ago,' said Aura behind her veil, 'all but the one who uglified me.'

'Then I should go to him,' said beautiful Belinda. 'Dress up as a beggar maid, and give him fifty pounds to do it. Not more, or he may suspect that you're not a beggar maid. It will be great fun. I'd go with you only I promised Bellamant faithfully that I'd be home to lunch.' And off she went in her mother-of-pearl coach, leaving Aura to look through the bound volumes of *The Perfect Lady* in the palace library, to find out the proper costume for a beggar maid.

Now that very morning the Magician's old nurse had packed up a ham and some eggs and some honey and some apples and a sweet bunch of old-fashioned flowers, and borrowed the baker's boy to hold the horse for her, and started off to see the Magician. It was forty years since she'd seen him, but she loved him still, and now she thought she could do him a good turn. She asked in the town for his address, and learned that he lived in the Black Tower.

'But you'd best be careful,' the townsfolk said; 'he's a spiteful chap.'

'Bless you,' said the old nurse, 'he won't hurt me as I nursed him when he was a babe, in a plaid frock with the dearest little fat legs you ever did see.'

So she got to the tower, and the guards let her through. Taykin was almost pleased to see her – remember he had had no visitors for twenty years –

and he was quite pleased to see the ham and the honey.

'But where did I put them heggs?' said the nurse, 'and the apples – I must have left them at home after all.'

She had. But the Magician just waved his hand in the air, and there was a basket of apples that hadn't been there before. The eggs he took out of her bonnet, the folds of her shawl, and even from his own mouth, just like a conjuror does. Only of course he was a real Magician.

'Lor!' said she, 'it's like magic.'

'It is magic,' said he. 'That's my trade. It's quite a pleasure to have an audience again. I've lived here alone for twenty years. It's very lonely, especially of an evening.'

'Can't you get out?' said the nurse.

'No. King's orders must be respected, but it's a dog's life.' He sniffed, made himself a magic handkerchief out of empty air, and wiped his eyes.

'Take an apprentice, my dear,' said the nurse.

'And teach him my magic? Not me.'

'Suppose you got one so stupid he couldn't learn?'

'That would be all right – but it's no use advertising for a stupid person – you'd get no answers.'

'You needn't advertise,' said the nurse; and she went out and brought in James, who was really the Prince of the Fortunate Islands, and also the baker's boy she had brought with her to hold the horse's head.

'Now, James,' she said, 'you'd like to be apprenticed, wouldn't you?'

'Yes,' said the poor stupid boy.

'Then give the gentleman your money, James.'

James did.

'My last doubts vanish,' said the Magician, 'he is stupid. Nurse, let us celebrate the occasion with a little drop of something. Not before the boy because of setting an example. James, wash up. Not here, silly: in the back kitchen.'

So James washed up, and as he was very clumsy he happened to break a little bottle of essence of dreams that was on the shelf, and instantly there floated up from the washing-up water the vision of a princess more beautiful than the day – so beautiful that even James could not help seeing how beautiful she was, and holding out his arms to her as she came floating through the air above the kitchen sink. But when he held out his arms she vanished. He sighed and washed up harder than ever.

'I wish I wasn't so stupid,' he said and then there was a knock at the door. James wiped his hands and opened. Someone stood there in very picturesque rags and tatters. 'Please,' said someone, who was of course the Princess, 'is Professor Taykin at home?'

'Walk in, please,' said James.

'My snakes alive!' said Taykin, 'what a day we're having. Three visitors in one morning. How kind of you to call. Won't you take a chair?'

'I hoped,' said the veiled Princess, 'that you'd give me something else to take.'

'A glass of wine,' said Taykin. 'You'll take a glass of wine?'

'No, thank you,' said the beggar maid who was the Princess.

'Then take . . . take your veil off,' said the nurse, 'or you won't feel the benefit of it when you go out.'

'I can't,' said Aura, 'it wouldn't be safe.'

'Too beautiful, eh?' said the Magician. 'Still – you're quite safe here.'

'Can you do magic?' she abruptly asked.

'A little,' said he ironically.

'Well,' said she, 'it's like this. I'm so ugly no one can bear to look at me. And I want to go as kitchen-maid to the palace. They want a cook and a scullion and a kitchen-maid. I thought perhaps you'd give me something to make me pretty. I'm only a poor beggar maid . . . it would be a great thing to me if . . . '

'Go along with you,' said Taykin, very cross indeed. 'I never give to beggars.'

'Here's twopence,' whispered poor James, pressing it into her hand, 'it's all I've got left.'

'Thank you,' she whispered back. 'You are good.'

And to the Magician she said:

'I happen to have fifty pounds. I'll give it you for a new face.'

'Done,' cried Taykin. 'Here's another stupid one!' He grabbed the money, waved his wand, and then and there before the astonished eyes of the nurse and the apprentice the ugly beggar maid became the loveliest princess in the world.

'Lor!' said the nurse.

'My dream!' cried the apprentice.

'Please,' said the Princess, 'can I have a looking-glass?' The apprentice ran to unhook the one that hung over the kitchen sink, and handed it to her. 'Oh,' she said, 'how very pretty I am. How can I thank you?'

'Quite easily,' said the Magician, 'beggar maid as you are, I hereby offer you my hand and heart.'

He put his hand into his waistcoat and pulled out his heart. It was fat and pink, and the Princess did not like the look of it.

'Thank you very much,' said she, 'but I'd rather not.'

'But I insist,' said Taykin.

'But really, your offer . . . '

'Most handsome, I'm sure,' said the nurse.

'My affections are engaged,' said the Princess, looking down. 'I can't marry you.'

'Am I to take this as a refusal?' asked Taykin; and the Princess said she feared that he was.

'Very well, then,' he said, 'I shall see you home, and ask your father about it. He'll not let you refuse an offer like this. Nurse, come and tie my necktie.'

So he went out, and the nurse with him.

Then the Princess told the apprentice in a very great hurry who she was.

95

'It would never do,' she said, 'for him to see me home. He'd find out that I was the Princess, and he'd uglify me again in no time.'

'He shan't see you home,' said James. 'I may be stupid but I'm strong too.'

'How brave you are,' said Aura admiringly, 'but I'd rather slip away quietly, without any fuss. Can't you undo the patent lock of that door?' The apprentice tried but he was too stupid, and the Princess was not strong enough.

'I'm sorry,' said the apprentice who was a prince. 'I can't undo the door, but when he does I'll hold him and you can get away. I dreamed of you this morning,' he added.

'I dreamed of you too,' said she, 'but you were different.'

'Perhaps,' said poor James sadly, 'the person you dreamed about wasn't stupid, and I am.'

'Are you really?' cried the Princess. 'I am so glad!'

'That's rather unkind, isn't it?' said he.

'No; because if that's all that makes you different from the man I dreamed about I can soon make that all right.'

And with that she put her hands on his shoulders and kissed him. And at her kiss his stupidness passed away like a cloud, and he became as clever as anyone need be; and besides knowing all the ordinary lessons he would have learned if he had stayed at home in his palace, he knew all the geography of his father's kingdom, and the exports and imports and the conditions of politics. And he knew also that the Princess loved him.

So he caught her in his arms and kissed her, and they were very happy, and told each other over and over again what a beautiful world it was, and how wonderful it was that they should have found each other, seeing that the world is not only beautiful but rather large.

'That first one was a magic kiss, you know,' said she. 'My fairy godmother gave it to me, and I've been keeping it all these years for you. You must get away from here and come to the palace. Oh, you'll manage it – you're clever now.'

'Yes,' he said, 'I am clever now. I can undo the lock for you. Go, my dear, go before he comes back.'

So the Princess went. And only just in time; for as she went out of one door Taykin came in at the other.

He was furious to find her gone; and I should not like to write down the things he said to his apprentice when he found that James had been so stupid as to open the door for her. They were not polite things at all.

He tried to follow her. But the Princess had warned the guards, and he could not get out.

'Oh,' he cried, 'if only my old magic would work outside this tower. I'd soon be even with her.'

And then in a strange, confused, yet quite sure way, he felt that the spell that held him, the White Witch's spell, was dissolved.

'To the palace!' he cried; and rushing to the

cauldron that hung over the fire he leaped into it, leaped out in the form of a red lion, and disappeared.

Without a moment's hesitation the Prince, who was his apprentice, followed him, calling out the same words and leaping into the same cauldron, while the poor nurse screamed and wrung her hands. As he touched the liquor in the cauldron he felt that he was not quite himself. He was, in fact, a green dragon. He felt himself vanish – a most uncomfortable sensation – and reappeared, with a suddenness that took his breath away, in his own form and at the back door of the palace.

The time had been short, but already the Magician had succeeded in obtaining an engagement as palace cook. How he did it without references I don't know. Perhaps he made the references by magic as he had made the eggs and the apples and the handkerchief.

Taykin's astonishment and annoyance at being followed by his faithful apprentice were soon soothed, for he saw that a stupid scullion would be of great use. Of course, he had no idea that James had been made clever by a kiss.

'But how are you going to cook?' asked the apprentice. 'You don't know how!'

'I shall cook,' said Taykin, 'as I do everything else – by magic.' And he did. I wish I had time to tell you how he turned out a hot dinner of seventeen courses from totally empty saucepans, how James looked in a cupboard for spices and found it empty, and how next moment the nurse walked out of it. The

Magician had been so long alone that he seemed to revel in the luxury of showing off to someone, and he leaped about from one cupboard to another, produced cats and cockatoos out of empty jars, and made mice and rabbits disappear and reappear till James's head was in a whirl, for all his cleverness; and the nurse, as she washed up, wept tears of pure joy at her boy's wonderful skill.

'All this excitement's bad for my heart, though,' Taykin said at last, and pulling his heart out of his chest, he put it on a shelf, and as he did so his magic notebook fell from his breast and the apprentice picked it up. Taykin did not see him do it; he was busy making the kitchen lamp fly about the room like a pigeon.

It was just then that the Princess came in, looking more lovely than ever in a simple little morning frock of white chiffon and diamonds.

'The beggar maid,' said Taykin, 'looking like a princess! I'll marry her just the same.'

'I've come to give the orders for dinner,' she said; and then she saw who it was, and gave one little cry and stood still, trembling.

'To order the dinner,' said the nurse. 'Then you're – '

'Yes,' said Aura, 'I'm the Princess.'

'You're the Princess,' said the Magician. 'Then I'll marry you all the more. And if you say no I'll uglify you as the word leaves your lips. Oh yes – you think I've just been amusing myself over my cooking – but

99

I've really been brewing the strongest spell in the world. Marry me – or drink – '

The Princess shuddered at these dreadful words.

'Drink, or marry me,' said the Magician. 'If you marry me you shall be beautiful for ever.'

'Ah,' said the nurse, 'he's a match even for a Princess.'

'I'll tell papa,' said the Princess, sobbing.

'No you won't,' said Taykin. 'Your father will never know. If you won't marry me you shall drink this and become my scullery maid – my hideous scullery maid – and wash up for ever in the lonely tower.'

He caught her by the wrist.

'Stop!' cried the apprentice who was a prince.

'Stop? Me? Nonsense! Pooh!' said the Magician.

'Stop, I say!' said James, who was Fortunatus. 'I've got your heart!' He had – and he held it up in one hand, and in the other a cooking knife.

'One step nearer that lady,' said he, 'and in goes the knife.'

The Magician positively skipped in his agony and terror.

'I say, look out!' he cried. 'Be careful what you're doing. Accidents happen so easily! Suppose your foot slipped! Then no apologies would meet the case. That's my heart you've got there. My life's bound up in it.'

'I know. That's often the case with people's hearts,' said Fortunatus. 'We've got you, my dear sir, on

100

toast. My Princess, might I trouble you to call the guards.'

The Magician did not dare to resist, so the guards arrested him. The nurse, though in floods of tears,

101

managed to serve up a very good plain dinner, and after dinner the Magician was brought before the King.

Now the King, as soon as he had seen that his daughter had been made so beautiful, had caused a large number of princes to be fetched by telephone. He was anxious to get her married at once in case she turned ugly again. So before he could do justice to the Magician he had to settle which of the princes was to marry the Princess. He had chosen the Prince of the Diamond Mountains, a very nice steady young man with a good income. But when he suggested the match to the Princess she declined it, and the Magician, who was standing at the foot of the throne steps loaded with chains, clattered forward and said:

'Your Majesty, will you spare my life if I tell you something you don't know?'

The King, who was a very inquisitive man, said 'Yes.'

'Then know,' said Taykin, 'that the Princess won't marry your choice because she's made one of her own – my apprentice.'

The Princess meant to have told her father this when she had got him alone and in a good temper. But now he was in a bad temper, and in full audience.

The apprentice was dragged in, and all the Princess's agonized pleadings only got this out of the King:

102

'All right. I won't hang him. He shall be best man at your wedding.'

Then the King took his daughter's hand and set her in the middle of the hall, and set the Prince of the Diamond Mountains on her right and the apprentice on her left. Then he said:

'I will spare the life of this aspiring youth on your left if you'll promise never to speak to him again, and if you'll promise to marry the gentleman on your right before tea this afternoon.'

The wretched Princess looked at her lover and his lips formed the word 'Promise'.

So she said, 'I promise never to speak to the gentleman on my left and to marry the gentleman on my right before tea today,' and held out her hand to the Prince of the Diamond Mountains.

Then suddenly, in the twinkling of an eye, the Prince of the Diamond Mountains was on her left, and her hand was held by her own Prince, who stood at her right hand. And yet nobody seemed to have moved. It was the purest and most high-class magic.

'Dished,' cried the King, 'absolutely dished!'

'A mere trifle,' said the apprentice modestly. 'I've got Taykin's magic recipe book, as well as his heart.'

'Well, we must make the best of it, I suppose,' said the King crossly. 'Bless you, my children.'

He was less cross when it was explained to him that the apprentice was really the Prince of the Fortunate Islands, and a much better match than the Prince of the Diamond Mountains, and he was in quite a good temper by the time the nurse threw herself in front of the throne and begged the King to let the Magician off altogether – chiefly on the ground that when he was a baby he was the dearest little duck that ever was, in the prettiest plaid frock, with the loveliest fat legs.

The King, moved by these arguments, said:

'I'll spare him if he'll promise to be good.'

'You will, ducky, won't you?' said the nurse, crying.

'No,' said the Magician, 'I won't; and what's more, I can't.'

The Princess, who was now so happy that she wanted everyone else to be happy too, begged her lover to make Taykin good 'by magic'.

'Alas, my dearest lady,' said the Prince, 'no one can be made good by magic. I could take the badness out of him – there's an excellent recipe in this note-book – but if I did that there'd be so little left.'

'Every little helps,' said the nurse wildly.

Prince Fortunatus, who was James, who was the apprentice, studied the book for a few moments, and then said a few words in a language no one present had ever heard before.

As he spoke the wicked Magician began to tremble and shrink.

'Oh, my boy – be good! Promise you'll be good,' cried the nurse, still in tears.

The Magician seemed to be shrinking inside his clothes. He grew smaller and smaller. The nurse caught him in her arms, and still he grew less and less, till she seemed to be holding nothing but a bundle of clothes. Then with a cry of love and triumph she tore the Magician's clothes away and held up a chubby baby boy, with the very plaid frock and fat legs she had so often and so lovingly described.

'I said there wouldn't be much of him when his badness was out,' said the Prince Fortunatus.

'I will be good; oh, I will,' said the baby boy that had been the Magician.

'I'll see to that,' said the nurse. And so the story ends with love and a wedding, and showers of white roses.

# The Elephant's Child

In the High and Far-Off Times the Elephant, O Best
Beloved, had no trunk. He had only a blackish, bulgy
nose, as big as a boot, that he could wriggle about
from side to side; but he couldn't pick up things with
it. But there was one Elephant – a new Elephant –
an Elephant's Child – who was full of 'satiable curtiosity, and that means he asked ever so many questions. And he lived in Africa, and he filled all Africa
with his 'satiable curtiosities. He asked his tall aunt,
the Ostrich, why her tail-feathers grew just so, and
his tall aunt, the Ostrich, spanked him with her hard,
hard claw. He asked his tall uncle, the Giraffe, what
made his skin spotty, and his tall uncle, the Giraffe,
spanked him with his hard, hard hoof. And still he
was full of 'satiable curtiosity! He asked his broad
aunt, the Hippopotamus, why her eyes were red,
and his broad aunt, the Hippopotamus, spanked him
with her broad, broad hoof; and he asked his hairy
uncle, the Baboon, why melons tasted just so, and
his hairy uncle, the Baboon, spanked him with his
hairy, hairy paw. And still he was full of 'satiable

curtiosity! He asked questions about everything that he saw, or heard, or felt, or smelt, or touched, and all his uncles and aunts spanked him. And still he was full of 'satiable curtiosity!

One fine morning in the middle of the Precession of the Equinoxes this 'satiable Elephant's Child asked a new fine question that he had never asked before. He asked, 'What does the Crocodile have for dinner?' Then everybody said, 'Hush!' in a loud and dretful tone, and they spanked him immediately and directly, without stopping, for a long time.

By and by, when that was finished, he came upon Kolokolo Bird sitting in the middle of a wait-a-bit thorn-bush, and he said, 'My father has spanked me, and my mother has spanked me; all my aunts and uncles have spanked me for my 'satiable curtiosity; and still I want to know what the Crocodile has for dinner!'

Then the Kolokolo Bird said, with a mournful cry, 'Go to the banks of the great, grey-green, greasy Limpopo River, all set about with fever-trees, and find out.'

That very next morning, when there was nothing left of the Equinoxes, because the Precession had preceded according to precedent, this 'satiable Elephant's Child took a hundred pounds of sugar-cane (the long purple kind), and seventeen melons (the greeny-crackly kind), and said to all his dear families, 'Good-bye, I am going to the great, grey-green, greasy Limpopo River, all set about with fever-trees, to find out what the Crocodile has for dinner.' And they all spanked him once more for luck, though he asked them most politely to stop.

Then he went away, a little warm, but not at all astonished, eating melons, and throwing the rind about, because he could not pick it up.

He went from Graham's Town to Kimberley, and from Kimberley to Khama's Country, and from Khama's Country he went east by north, eating melons all the time, till at last he came to the banks of the great, grey-green, greasy Limpopo River, all set about with fever-trees, precisely as Kolokolo Bird had said.

Now, you must know and understand, O Best Beloved, that till that very week, and day, and hour, and minute, this 'satiable Elephant's Child had never seen a Crocodile, and did not know what one was like. It was all his 'satiable curtiosity.

The first thing he found was a Bi-Coloured-Python-Rock-Snake, curled round a rock.

' 'Scuse me,' said the Elephant's Child most politely, 'but have you seen such a thing as a Crocodile in these promiscuous parts?'

'Have I seen a Crocodile?' said the Bi-Coloured-Python-Rock-Snake, in a voice of dretful scorn. 'What will you ask me next?'

' 'Scuse me,' said the Elephant's Child, 'but could you kindly tell me what he has for dinner?'

Then the Bi-Coloured-Python-Rock-Snake uncoiled himself very quickly from the rock, and spanked the Elephant's Child with his scalesome, flailsome tail.

'That is odd,' said the Elephant's Child, 'because my father and my mother, and my uncle and my aunt, not to mention my other aunt, the Hippopotamus, and my other uncle, the Baboon, have all spanked me for my 'satiable curtiosity – and I suppose this is the same thing.'

So he said good-bye very politely to the Bi-Coloured-Python-Rock-Snake, and helped to coil him up on the rock again, and went on, a little warm, but not at all astonished, eating melons, and throwing the rind about, because he could not pick it up, till he trod on what he thought was a log of wood at the very edge of the great, grey-green, greasy Limpopo River, all set about with fever-trees.

But it was really the Crocodile, O Best Beloved, and the Crocodile winked one eye – like this!

' 'Scuse me,' said the Elephant's Child most politely, 'but do you happen to have seen a Crocodile in these promiscuous parts?'

Then the Crocodile winked the other eye, and lifted half his tail out of the mud; and the Elephant's Child stepped back most politely, because he did not wish to be spanked again.

'Come hither, Little One,' said the Crocodile. 'Why do you ask such things?'

' 'Scuse me,' said the Elephant's Child most politely, 'but my father has spanked me, my mother has spanked me, not to mention my tall aunt, the

109

Ostrich, and my tall uncle, the Giraffe who can kick ever so hard, as well as my broad aunt, the Hippopotamus, and my hairy uncle, the Baboon, and including the Bi-Coloured-Python-Rock-Snake, with the scalesome, flailsome tail, just up the bank, who spanks harder than any of them; and so, if it's quite all the same to you, I don't want to be spanked any more.'

'Come hither, Little One,' said the Crocodile, 'for I am the Crocodile,' and he wept crocodile-tears to show it was quite true.

Then the Elephant's Child grew all breathless, and panted, and kneeled down on the bank and said, 'You are the very person I have been looking for all these long days. Will you please tell me what you have for dinner?'

'Come hither, Little One,' said the Crocodile, 'and I'll whisper.'

Then the Elephant's Child put his head down close to the Crocodile's musky, tusky mouth, and the Crocodile caught him by his little nose, which up to that very week, day, hour, and minute, had been no bigger than a boot, though much more useful.

'I think,' said the Crocodile – and he said it between his teeth, like this – 'I think today I will begin with Elephant's Child!'

At this, O Best Beloved, the Elephant's Child was much annoyed, and he said, speaking through his nose, like this, 'Led go! You are hurtig be!'

Then the Bi-Coloured-Python-Rock-Snake scuffed

down from the bank and said, 'My young friend, if you do not now, immediately and instantly, pull as hard as ever you can, it is my opinion that your acquaintance in the large-pattern leather ulster' (and by this he meant the Crocodile) 'will jerk you into yonder limpid stream before you can say Jack Robinson.'

This is the way Bi-Coloured-Python-Rock-Snakes always talk.

Then the Elephant's Child sat back on his little haunches, and pulled, and pulled, and his nose began to stretch. And the Crocodile floundered into the water, making it all creamy with great sweeps of his tail, and he pulled, and pulled, and pulled.

And the Elephant's Child's nose kept on stretching; and the Elephant's Child spread all his little four legs and pulled, and pulled, and pulled, and his nose kept on stretching; and the Crocodile threshed his tail like an oar, and he pulled, and pulled, and pulled, and at each pull the Elephant's Child's nose grew longer and longer – and it hurt him hijjus!

Then the Elephant's Child felt his legs slipping, and he said through his nose, which was now nearly five feet long, 'This is too butch for be!'

Then the Bi-Coloured-Python-Rock-Snake came down from the bank, and knotted himself in a double-clove-hitch round the Elephant's Child's hind-legs, and said, 'Rash and inexperienced traveller, we will now seriously devote ourselves to a little high tension, because if we do not, it is my

impression that yonder self-propelling man-of-war
with the armour-plated upper deck' (and by this, O
Best Beloved, he meant the Crocodile) 'will perma-
nently vitiate your future career.'

That is the way all Bi-Coloured-Python-Rock-
Snakes always talk.

So he pulled, and the Elephant's Child pulled, and
the Crocodile pulled; but the Elephant's Child and
the Bi-Coloured-Python-Rock-Snake pulled hardest;
and at last the Crocodile let go of the Elephant's

Child's nose with a plop that you could hear all up and down the Limpopo.

Then the Elephant's Child sat down most hard and sudden; but first he was careful to say 'Thank you' to the Bi-Coloured-Python-Rock-Snake; and next he was kind to his poor pulled nose, and wrapped it all up in cool banana leaves, and hung it in the great, grey-green, greasy Limpopo to cool.

'What are you doing that for?' said the Bi-Coloured-Python-Rock-Snake.

' 'Scuse me,' said the Elephant's Child, 'but my nose is badly out of shape, and I am waiting for it to shrink.'

'Then you will have to wait a long time,' said the Bi-Coloured-Python-Rock-Snake. 'Some people do not know what is good for them.'

The Elephant's Child sat there for three days waiting for his nose to shrink. But it never grew any shorter, and, besides, it made him squint. For, O Best Beloved, you will see and understand that the Crocodile had pulled it out into a really truly trunk same as all Elephants have today.

At the end of the third day a fly came and stung him on the shoulder, and before he knew what he was doing he lifted up his trunk and hit that fly dead with the end of it.

'Vantage number one!' said the Bi-Coloured-Python-Rock-Snake. 'You couldn't have done that with a mere-smear nose. Try and eat a little now.'

Before he thought what he was doing the

Elephant's Child put out his trunk and plucked a large bundle of grass, dusted it clean against his forelegs, and stuffed it into his own mouth.

'Vantage number two!' said the Bi-Coloured-Python-Rock-Snake. 'You couldn't have done that with a mere-smear nose. Don't you think the sun is very hot here?'

'It is,' said the Elephant's Child, and before he thought what he was doing he schlooped up a sch-loop of mud from the banks of the great, grey-green, greasy Limpopo, and slapped it on his head, where it made a cool schloopy-sloshy mud-cap all trickly behind his ears.

'Vantage number three!' said the Bi-Coloured-Python-Rock-Snake. 'You couldn't have done that with a mere-smear nose. Now how do you feel about being spanked again?'

' 'Scuse me,' said the Elephant's Child, 'but I should not like it at all.'

'How would you like to spank somebody?' said the Bi-Coloured-Python-Rock-Snake.

'I should like it very much indeed,' said the Elephant's Child.

'Well,' said the Bi-Coloured-Python-Rock-Snake, 'you will find that new nose of yours very useful to spank people with.'

'Thank you,' said the Elephant's Child, 'I'll remember that; and now I think I'll go home to all my dear families and try.'

So the Elephant's Child went home across Africa

frisking and whisking his trunk. When he wanted fruit to eat he pulled fruit down from a tree, instead of waiting for it to fall as he used to do. When he wanted grass he plucked grass up from the ground, instead of going on his knees as he used to do. When the flies bit him he broke off the branch of a tree and used it as a fly-whisk; and he made himself a new, cool, slushy-squshy mud-cap whenever the sun was hot. When he felt lonely walking through Africa he sang to himself down his trunk, and the noise was louder than several brass bands. He went specially out of his way to find a broad Hippopotamus (she was no relation of his), and he spanked her very hard, to make sure that the Bi-Coloured-Python-Rock-Snake had spoken the truth about his new trunk. The rest of the time he picked up the melon-rinds that he had dropped on his way to the Limpopo – for he was a Tidy Pachyderm.

One dark evening he came back to all his dear families, and he coiled up his trunk and said, 'How do you do?' They were very glad to see him, and immediately said, 'Come here and be spanked for your 'satiable curtiosity.'

'Pooh,' said the Elephant's Child. 'I don't think you peoples know anything about spanking; but I do, and I'll show you.'

Then he uncurled his trunk and knocked two of his dear brothers head over heels.

'O Bananas!' said they, 'where did you learn that trick, and what have you done to your nose?'

'I got a new one from the Crocodile on the banks of the great, grey-green, greasy Limpopo River,' said the Elephant's Child. 'I asked him what he had for dinner, and he gave me this to keep.'

'It looks very ugly,' said his hairy uncle, the Baboon.

'It does,' said the Elephant's Child. 'But it's very useful,' and he picked up his hairy uncle, the Baboon, by one hairy leg, and hove him into a hornet's nest.

Then that bad Elephant's Child spanked all his dear families for a long time, till they were very warm and greatly astonished. He pulled out his tall Ostrich aunt's tail-feathers; and he caught his tall uncle, the Giraffe, by the hind-leg, and dragged him through a thorn-bush; and he shouted at his broad aunt, the Hippopotamus, and blew bubbles into her ear when she was sleeping in the water after meals; but he never let any one touch Kolokolo Bird.

At last things grew so exciting that his dear families went off one by one in a hurry to the banks of the great, grey-green, greasy Limpopo River, all set about with fever-trees, to borrow new noses from the Crocodile. When they came back nobody spanked anybody any more, and ever since that day, O Best Beloved, all the Elephants you will ever see, besides all those that you won't, have trunks precisely like the trunk of the 'satiable Elephant's Child.